BLURB

Bob "Mac" Mackenzie has finally started construction on the house of his dreams. The lakeside paradise is everything he imagined, except for the nightmare next door. The pretty project manager always apologizes for the inconveniences her build is causing, but the accidents keep happening.

The Holiday Beach mansion she designed was supposed to be the diamond in architect Lori Baker's crown, but instead, she's wearing dirt on her face. Impossible clients are driving her to the brink, and a few initial misunderstandings with the handsome neighbor have turned every interaction into an all-out war.

When Lori is fired after she tries to fix the damage the owners cause to Mac's property, she finds herself stranded and jobless. With nothing to go home to, Holiday Beach could be the perfect place to start over on her own Independence Day. All she needs is a chance to showcase her skills—but her best shot means working with her worst enemy.

CHAPTER 1

THE ONLY GOOD thing about working on a new summer home build on Star Lake was the fact Lori Baker got to stop in Holiday Beach for the best coffee in the state every time she made the three-hour trip from Minneapolis to deal with the project of doom.

By the Cup was a small, independent coffee shop that faced the public beach. It wasn't busy at this point in early May, but Lori could picture the lines going out the door once the summer tourist crowds descended on the resort town. The coffee was delicious, the location convenient, and the staff friendly—if you weren't known around town as "that woman working on the house next to Mac's."

She had made some missteps when she'd first arrived in Holiday Beach. She was used to taking a heavy-handed approach to contractors and suppliers in the city. That didn't fly in a small town. Lori knew that now. But it was too little, too late. Her reputation was shot. All she could do was try to be friendly where she could. Like in the coffee shop.

As she was paying, she noticed a sign in the baking display case. "What is the Green, White, and Blue Fund?" she asked.

The quiet barista behind the counter blinked at the question. "The Holiday Beach Parks Committee is running a raffle to raise funds to install new garbage and recycling bins around town to help keep the beach and parks clean this summer. The drawing is this weekend."

"I'm all for clean beaches. That sounds like a great initiative. I'll take two tickets, please."

She got her first smile in three visits. "That's terrific," the brunette said. "Here, use my pen. I'm Rachel."

Lori dutifully filled in her name, address, email, and phone number. "Thanks, Rachel. What's the prize?"

"A weekend at the Dew Drop Inn. It's the hotel on the edge of town."

"The one with the amazing stained-glass window facing the highway?"

"That's the one."

"Wouldn't that be a treat!" Lori drove past that hotel on every trip. The window glowed like a beacon, inviting travellers to come and stay for a while. Unfortunately for her, the company had only sprung for the Fairlaine Motel up the highway on the rare occasion she'd needed to spend the night.

Rachel handed over her tickets, but Lori was already at the door when she realized she'd been given three. "You gave me an extra ticket."

"No, that's for you. Earlier this morning, a customer paid for a ticket and told me to give it to the next person who bought one."

"Why?"

Rachel shrugged. "Lucy has a whole explanation

about how her strange luck works, but it doesn't matter. All three are yours. The drawing is tomorrow, so keep your phone handy in case you win."

"Thanks." Lori stuffed the tickets into the bottom of her purse, where she'd find them in a few months to toss them in the trash. Despite how attractive the town looked on the outside, it would never be lucky for her.

Holiday Beach was a charming little place. According to the research she'd done, a few years earlier the town had decided to build on its name and market itself as a holiday destination, using every special date on the calendar as a reason to come to Holiday Beach and celebrate.

Lori had arrived for the first time in December and found a magical winter wonderland. Every house, business, and building sparkled in lights and decorations. Most were for Christmas, but with so many holidays in December and early January, Lori had counted at least four different celebrations. The town was awash in red hearts and winged cupids for Valentine's Day and then shifted immediately to St. Patrick's Day green. She'd especially enjoyed Easter earlier in April because, in addition to the decorations, Mother Nature got into the act and sprinkled blooming crocuses and tulips all over the place.

Next on the calendar was Memorial Day. It was only the last week of April, but people had already started preparing their yards for a sunny season of outdoor living. They moved summer furniture out of sheds, hung patio lights, and brought out their flags now that the weather wouldn't treat them as badly. Lori had seen posters for a service to be held on the last Monday of May.

It was a short trip from the coffee shop to the

construction site. She had to drive past Mac Mackenzie's driveway. The house that had started to go up at the same time as the Parkmans' had progressed a lot over the past month. She started to mentally track the changes, but quickly abandoned the thought when her project came into view.

At least, it used to be her project.

Lori had toiled away for two years as a junior associate at Turner Architecture Group, taking whatever projects she'd been given. Then *Modern Minnesota* magazine announced a contest for new environmentally friendly buildings, and Lori's boss allowed her to enter under the company's name.

They threw her a party when her design made the top ten. It also encouraged her bosses to let her take the important step of approaching her own clients to bring in new business.

The Parkmans saw her design in the magazine and told her boss they wanted it for their new summer property in Holiday Beach. He assigned Lori as the architect in charge of the project.

The first time Lori arrived at the build site, she found twin stone pillars already constructed at the base of the double-wide driveway. Mr. and Mrs. Parkman informed her all the homes on Shakespeare Drive had literary names, but they had not yet been inspired by her design.

She should have taken that as a sign.

Her prize-winning design was supposed to be a stepping-stone to a new and glorious phase of her career. Instead, it had turned into a weight around her neck, determined to pull her into a pit of despair and frustration. The Parkmans replaced every green appliance choice with something bigger or more powerful. Then they nixed all products made from renewable resources, saying they weren't as pretty as other options. And those were just the smallest changes to her original design. They began demanding bigger, grander additions. It wasn't long before the only green thing left was the money it was costing to build it.

The only reason Lori had to come out to the project as often as she did was because the clients continually insisted on increasing the scope of work. She had no idea what surprise was in store for this trip. All Mrs. Parkman said was she had "an exciting new project" to share and Lori had to come to Holiday Beach immediately.

"Where is Mrs. Parkman?" Lori asked the first contractor she saw.

"The solarium."

The solarium—two-hundred square feet with glass walls and a glass ceiling—had been Mrs. Parkman's most recent last-minute alteration to the plans. They were scheduled to pour the foundation that day. Lori thumped through the house in her work boots and found her client watching a workman in the distance.

"Laura, I'm so glad you could make it. We had a terrific idea the other night. Since we weren't able to get the lakefront property we wanted and the public beach is two miles away, we've decided to put in a pool!"

"It's Lori or Lorelei, Mrs. Parkman. And did you say a pool?" Lori repeated.

The demanding redhead clapped in excitement. "In ground. Heated, of course. With a lovely, large patio and a pool house with a shower and maybe a small kitchen area for snacks."

"A pool and a pool house?"

"We've already called Tidal Pools to come out. I know

this will mean more permits and changes, but you've managed so far. I have the perfect location picked out. Just far enough from the house so the noise won't be an issue, but not too long of a walk." Mrs. Parkman pointed to the treeline that separated her property from Mac Mackenzie's. "That spruce has to go. It'll block the afternoon sun. I've sent someone out to take care of it."

"The tall spruce that's ringed by the birch trees?" Lori asked.

"Yes, exactly. You know what? I think you're right. Those birches will have to come down too. I don't want their leaves clogging the filter in the fall."

Lori bolted.

CHAPTER 2

Bob "Mac" Mackenzie sipped flawlessly brewed coffee as he sat on his deck, looking out over Star Lake on a beautiful April afternoon. Life didn't get much better than this. Granted, the coffee was from By the Cup and in a travel mug because his kitchen cupboards hadn't arrived yet. He was sitting in a folding lawn chair with his back to the wall because the deck didn't have any railings and it was a long drop. Since he'd never be able to afford shorefront property, the view of the lake was through a gap in the trees across the road. But the sky was blue, the sun was shining, and the first robins of the year had returned to the cluster of poplars at the end of his driveway. Overall, the day was bordering on perfection.

It was a weekday morning. He should be at his current work site, repainting an empty office in the Holiday Beach Business Center with his partner. But his younger brother and partner at Mackenzie Brothers Painting was starting without him. Mac had to wait for the local building inspector to arrive to approve his electrical work so he could move on to the next phase of construction for his new home. The plans had been in the works for years, but it had been one delay after another. Mac had finally acquired the property the previous fall. But now it was all coming together.

The rumble of tires on gravel brought Mac to his feet. He recognized the truck, having seen it at several properties he'd worked on at his day job. "Hi, Murray."

"Hey, Mac. Is Lee's Cabin ready for this inspection?"

Mac had begun thinking of a name for his new home the second he'd made the offer for the property. He wasn't a huge reader, but there was one writer who had never let him down. He expected a lot of people to assume he was talking about another Lee and ask if the property had mockingbirds. He intended to correct his guests by saying it was home to a lot of superheroes. "Ready and confident," Mac said.

Drywall was stacked in the middle of what would be his living room. Boxes of flooring were in the dining room, and bathroom tiles waited upstairs in the master bedroom. The entire house was a glorified warehouse of specifically chosen materials and finishes. Today's electrical inspection was the last step out of his hands. If all went according to plan, Mac's home should be ready to move into by the end of June.

Murray didn't waste any time. He examined junction boxes, panels, and outlets, marking each with a check mark on his clipboard. "You are good to go, my friend."

Mac ran his fingers through his dark hair in relief. "Thanks a lot." He hadn't expected problems, but there was always the chance something could go wrong at the last minute.

"I'd stay for a tour, but I have a ton of places to go today. Another time?" his friend asked.

"Any time. Although I may end up putting you to work."

The inspector laughed. "I've been warned. Happy drywalling, Mac."

The annoying buzz of a chainsaw met them when they stepped outside. Both men looked at the half-constructed monstrosity in the lot next door. The new build was the bane of Mac's existence. Most of the other locals along Shakespeare Drive felt the same.

"Ah, yes, the Parkman project," Murray said with a grimace.

"Are they on your list for today?"

"Thankfully, no. That place is a nightmare. Sarah at the planning office pulls her hair out every time their name comes up."

The chainsaw almost drowned out his words. It sounded close. Dangerously close. After the confrontations he'd had with his new neighbors over the previous winter, Mac was quick to react. "You know what? I think I'd better check that out."

"Good luck, buddy."

Mac had specifically left a row of trees between the two properties rather than clear-cutting the area. It gave them both privacy and maintained a wind break around his house. The local wildlife also appreciated him protecting their natural habitats, although it had been a battle to keep the squirrels out of the attic until all the windows were installed. He came to a truce with them by constructing a feeder by the spruce tree that he could see from his primary bedroom window.

He was heading to that same spruce tree now, and it sounded like he was heading in the right direction. The chainsaw was getting louder. But now there was shouting as well. Most of it was muffled by the other noise, but two words in a familiar voice were clear. "No" and "stop."

Mac groaned, but he didn't stop moving. He had to see the latest disaster to be caused by Lorelei T. Baker. He didn't know if her middle initial was actually T, but he wouldn't be surprised if it was. The T was for Trouble because that's all she caused.

He didn't know the details of what was going on, but he was certain he could guess the result.

First, he'd find out what she'd done to mess up his construction plans. Like the time she'd told the driver to dump a truckload of lumber in the middle of his driveway until they could get to it.

Then she'd come over and apologize, claiming it was all a misunderstanding. It was what she did after a load of his windows was accidentally sent to his neighbor's address. Ms. Baker looked at the delivery, declared them to be entirely wrong, and sent them back to the manufacturer. What she didn't do was look at the invoice to verify they were her windows. When his windows hadn't arrived by their expected delivery date, he'd spent days tracking them down, only to discover they'd been returned to the factory. It took even longer to figure out how they got there. It put him two full weeks behind.

And then Lorelei Baker would promise it would never happen again. Like she had when her contractors trespassed on his property.

Mac forced himself to tamp down his irritation. That last one was an honest mistake and not at all what he assumed. Yes, there were people wandering around on his land, and yes, Lorelei invited them. But they were from the county zoning office and were there to mark the property line so nobody else would make another mistake.

Which he found out after he'd yelled at them. And Lorelei. But the other things had totally been her fault.

It took him a second to realize her shouting had stopped. The reason he hadn't noticed was because of the cracking and creaking of the pine tree. He blinked. He wasn't imagining things; it was getting closer. The treetop parted the two poplars closest to his house, and then the branches and trunk came into view, crashing through the thin undergrowth and crushing his brand-new squirrel feeder. The crown of the tree scraped the side of the house, ripping off rows of his brand-new siding.

"What is going on here?" he roared.

He plowed through the brush, uncaring of the branches whipping his face and tearing at his clothes. Lorelei Baker came into view first. Her already pale face went white when she saw him.

"Mac! Mr. Mackenzie, I am—" she began.

"Cutting down my trees!" Mac shouted. "It's not like this could be an accident, Ms. Baker. You had the area marked yourself. Then I put up a fence and caution tape and signs to ensure it didn't happen again. What went wrong?"

"I am so sor—"

His soon-to-be new neighbor, Mrs. Parkman, hurried behind the architect. "Mr. Mackenzie, what's happening here?"

"Your architect cut down one of my trees and it took down part of my house."

The woman in the pink hard hat pointed at his ring of four birch trees. "That spruce that was in this delightful little copse was on your property?"

"Yes. That's what the fence and the caution tape and the sign were for."

"There wasn't a fence or tape up when I got here," the man holding the chainsaw said. Mac recognized him and the look on his face. Poor Siggy wasn't lying. He didn't look surprised either; everyone in town had heard the stories about Lorelei Baker and the Parkmans too. Mac spied the pulled fence posts and a ball of caution tape just inside the Parkman's property line. But if Siggy said anything, the truth would put him in the hard spot of being between the person signing his paycheck and the townsfolk he'd have to live with after the job was over.

"Put the chainsaw back in its case, Siggy. Nobody will be cutting anything for a while. Let's everybody take a minute," Mac said, trying to keep his voice even. How was this even an issue? He couldn't have marked the property line any clearer.

"Mr. Mackenzie, I think this is just a misunderstanding. I told Laura I'd like to discuss making a change to the design. She just jumped the gun. No harm done."

"Except to my tree, my squirrel feeder, and my house," he said, interrupting.

"I didn't jump anything, Mr. Mackenzie," Lorelei protested.

"I'll have her explain what happened to your insurance company personally."

He was on a roll now. Even her own boss didn't like her. "Mrs. Parkman, I'm not going to put up with any more destruction of property or inconvenience because of your construction. I've tried to be understanding, but that ends now."

"I completely understand, Mr. Mackenzie, and I'm horrified you've had to tolerate it this long." The redheaded woman whirled on the source of all his troubles. "Laura, I insist you compensate Mr. Mackenzie for the damage you've caused."

"It's Lore-LEI," she said, emphasizing her name, "and I won't be compensating anybody for anything because I had nothing to do with any of this. I just got here."

"Laura...lie, go inside. Now."

It sounded like his least favorite architect was going to be taken to task. He hated when that happened to him. He'd been on the receiving end often enough as a contractor himself. But when something went wrong, it was up to him to make it right; letting the client yell first was part of fixing it. Lorelei Baker was about to learn that the hard way.

"Mac. Mr. Mackenzie, I just arrived. I had nothing to do with any of this. I especially didn't remove your fence or tell anybody to trespass. Not after what happened last time," she insisted.

"Laura, I'm tired of all your problems and excuses on this project. Perhaps we should part ways."

"Again, it's Lori or Lorelei, and you can't fire me over something you—"

"That's it! I think it would be best for you to leave," the older woman continued.

Shock. Anger. Disappointment. Mac recognized all the emotions playing across Lorelei's face. He almost felt bad for her. But he felt worse for his house.

"Please, Mrs. Parkman!"

"Now, Laura. While I can still give a half-decent report to your boss. Please don't bother Mr. Mackenzie with your excuses on your way out."

Lorelei nodded at Mrs. Parkman, lifted her chin, and picked her way across the rocky ground to her car. She stopped beside the driver's door. Looking at the trio again, she shook her head and then drove away without a word.

Mrs. Parkman made more noise about making sure he was compensated and apologizing again for her overambitious architect causing friction between the "soon-to-be neighbors and great friends."

Mac didn't fail to notice Siggy had remained silent throughout the entire exchange. "Come, Mr. Sigurdson. Let's let Mr. Mackenzie clean this up the way he wants it done."

Siggy hesitated when he grabbed his chainsaw. "It wasn't Lori," he mouthed silently.

A shiver struck him, and Mac couldn't help the feeling that getting Lorelei Baker out of his hair wasn't the win he thought it was.

CHAPTER 3

"FIRED?"

Lori wasn't sure if her grandmother was more shocked at her boss's response to the complaint against her, or if she was simply horrified a Baker had brought such disgrace onto their family name. Bakers did not get fired. They were loyal to their employers until they retired, which was how her grandmother was living in a very nice house on an even nicer pension after her grandfather's thirty-five years of service in the mayor's office in Minneapolis.

"Technically, I was downsized. I'll be able to claim unemployment insurance for a little while," Lori said. It also left her a small chance to get hired at another firm without a black mark on her job history.

"What happened?" her grandma demanded.

"I disagreed with the client."

"Lori, you know the client is always right. The Parkmans are friends of friends. You are responsible for your actions. Surely you can apologize and promise to do better next time."

The family pride song never changed. "Grandma, the client is not always right, and I am taking responsibility for my actions. What I refused to do was take responsibility for Mrs. Parkman's actions. I also refused the hefty bill for property damage her actions caused when I wasn't even there. I will not be played as a sucker, and no Baker should."

Don't let others take advantage of you was another verse the family liked to quote. The golden-haired, perfectly coiffed woman before her tapped her manicured nails on the table. "What are you going to do now?"

"I'm going to sleep in tomorrow morning and then start job hunting." It wasn't like she had any other options. Lori had worked at TAG since she'd graduated with her master's degree in architecture four years earlier. It had been a dream job. It wouldn't be easy to find another job with so much competition out there. She might have to compromise and just settle for a good position with a steady paycheck and decent hours. Not that Lori was about to disclose that to Mrs. Arlene Baker of the Minnesota Bakers.

"I could ask at bridge club if any members know of anyone looking for an architect. But you might want to do some reflecting to make sure you've identified the real source of the problem. After all, you've had a string of bad luck lately and the common denominator is you."

"Okay, I'll do that." It wasn't worth the energy to instigate another argument. Besides, her grandma would find a way to blame her for everything that had happened in the last couple of months. Like it was Lori's fault her eighteen-year-old cat passed away. Or her apartment building was converted into condos and put on the market at over a hundred thousand dollars more than she expected, so she couldn't buy it.

Her grandmother wasn't wrong about her string of bad luck, though. Things couldn't get much worse. She was living above her grandmother's garage. It was barely large enough for her and wouldn't have been big enough for a pet if Georgie had still been around. Still, Lori hadn't had the heart to get rid of the scarred scratching post missing all its rope wrappings after the cat she'd got on her eighth birthday had passed away in the spring.

She gave herself a shake. She couldn't afford to get bogged down with negativity. Lori had some good things going for her. She had a degree from a good school, the *Modern Minnesota* contest win, and four solid years of experience at a reputable company. That was a lot more than some people started with.

Lori fell asleep fully dressed after a pity party of frozen pizza and ice cream for one. The next morning, she was determined to start fresh. She jumped in the shower, poured herself a cup of coffee, and set her tablet on her tiny kitchen table. It was time to blitz her network and start sending emails to land herself a new job.

She had several waiting for her when she opened her inbox. She skipped two from friends that had "OMG" in the subject line; her news had evidently already started making the rounds. She deleted one with "You are the winner" and another offering her a BOGO sale at her favorite shoe store.

Then she paused. There was a second one from the "You are the winner" email address, only the subject line was different. "Sorry, that looked like spam. From By the Cup in Holiday Beach. You won—" The rest was cut off. She checked the sender and it looked like it belonged to the coffee shop it claimed to come from, so she carefully clicked.

"Hello, Lori Baker.

Thank you for purchasing a Green, White, and Blue raffle ticket to support keeping Holiday Beach clean by adding garbage cans and recycling bins to the boardwalk and local parks. We're pleased to tell you that you've won the grand prize of a two-night stay at the Dew Drop Inn. Please claim your prize at the email below so we can book your weekend getaway in Minnesota's premier holiday resort. Details and restrictions are noted on your ticket.

Sincerely, the Holiday Beach Parks Committee

She burst out laughing. Of course she'd won a trip to a town where she was universally hated. Why wouldn't she want to visit the place that ended her career?

Then she thought about it again.

She had absolutely nothing to lose going back there. She didn't have to follow any orders about asking local businesses for discounts or make invasive, expensive requests on behalf of her clients she knew were only going to alienate the Parkmans' soon-to-be neighbors.

She could walk into a store and pay full price and not have to try to haggle. Wouldn't that be a thrill! She owed the hardware store such a big apology for constantly asking for special pricing. Maybe she could buy what she needed to fix the garage's bathroom there and then drive the supplies home. It would be a small act of contrition, but it would give her a chance to apologize to the owner.

And it could be a chance for her to finally explore the

town. With spring in full bloom, she could walk along the beach, although it was still too cold to go swimming. She could check out one of the restaurant's patios. Lori couldn't remember the last time she'd had a real vacation where she didn't have her phone by her side.

She opened a new email and began typing her reply.

If this was legitimate, it could be exactly what she needed.

Her room overlooked the pool and the woods on the edge of the property. It was idyllic. Birds chirped in the trees. Fresh air blew through her open window, ruffling the curtains. Lori fell back onto the fluffy comforter and stretched out on the king-size mattress in the serene green room.

She was never leaving the Dew Drop Inn. The only thing missing was room service; the hotel didn't have an attached restaurant. Gloria Vargas, the assistant manager who'd checked her in, told her the bar next door offered snacks but no real food. Instead, she'd recommended a couple of restaurants in town that Lori intended to check out.

But first, she was going to sit in the sunshine on the pool deck and enjoy the peace and quiet. After the week she'd had, she deserved it. For three days, she'd updated her résumé, told everybody she knew she was looking for a new job, and reached out to all her professional contacts to see if there were any opportunities they knew of.

She'd received a slew of sympathy emails and exactly zero leads. At over a hundred times at bat, she struck out every single time. She never even made it to first base, which she considered to be an offer of an interview, let alone got the home run of a job offer.

"Enough," Lori said to herself. She grabbed her phone, earbuds, and water bottle. She was going to find a place in the sun where she could relax and listen to the Twins game and give herself a vacation from her life.

Her app tuned in during the second inning, and the Twins were ahead of the Royals by two at the end of the fifth. The bright but not yet powerful sun kept her cozy and warm until a cool breeze picked up. Lori looked away from the architecture of the hotel at a bank of blue-black clouds rolling in from the direction of the lake. It was barely visible over the roof of the building next door.

That's when she saw the scaffolding. She assumed it had always been there, but she hadn't paid any mind to the poles and planks on the far side of the shared parking lot. Now there was movement on it, drawing her attention. A stocky, dark-haired man scraped a strip of wood under the eaves, then moved down the wall to a fresh patch of paint. The metal scaffolding he stood on was about twelve feet in the air.

The figure became more entertaining as the minutes passed. After he was divebombed by a pair of sparrows, his hat flew off. As he grabbed for it, he knocked over a can of paint. When he stood, Lori got her first look at his face. She laughed out loud at the look of disgust on Mac Mackenzie's face when he realized he'd have to climb all the way down and back up again, lugging the pail. It couldn't happen to a more deserving guy.

Her amusement over, Lori returned her attention to the game. Half an inning later, a low rumble, barely audible, was followed by a particularly cold gust of air. She opened her eyes. The sun had disappeared behind a large black cloud. "Poolside game called on account of weather," Lori muttered as she grabbed her empty water bottle. A glance at her phone showed it was five o'clock. If she left now, she'd get the jump on the supper crowd at the restaurant Gloria recommended.

That was the last thought she had before a flash blinded her and a boom literally knocked her two steps back. When her sight returned, a spray of sparks and sparkles was flying off the roof next door. It looked like someone had set off a firework. Then her eye was drawn to a body dangling from a safety line off the scaffolding.

At first, she thought Mac had simply suffered another bout of clumsiness. The image of him dangling like a worm on a hook didn't make her feel bad in the slightest, since she was doing her own worm-dangling in the job market after their last interaction.

But then he didn't move.

The sliding glass door leading from the hotel to the pool deck slid open. "Are you alright? What was that?" Gloria asked. The dark-haired woman glanced around the pool area and sighed in relief. When Lori pointed at the smoking roof next door, the assistant manager gasped.

"You call the ambulance and fire department. I'll check on Mac," Lori said.

Gloria disappeared in a flash. Lori moved just as quickly. She didn't see any sparks or smoke coming from the scaffolding itself. She thought it was a good sign the hanging man wasn't smoking or sparking either. He was, however, groaning.

"Good, you're alive." She didn't expect an answer.

"Of course it's you. What did you do this time, Lorelei Baker?"

"That's not very welcoming for a man hanging upside

down off the side of a building." Since he was conscious and coherent, her urge to help was fading. She stepped over a paint can on its side, spilling brown stain onto the gravel path. "And, like the last time I saw you, I didn't do anything."

The banter was good. It let her know he wasn't too badly injured. If he was insulting her but not complaining about being in pain, it couldn't be too bad. "Do you want me to leave? Because I can go. I'm sure you'll be fine with all the blood rushing to your head and your elbow pointed in the wrong direction." As annoyed at him as she was, it was all talk. She'd never abandon an injured person. But she wasn't going to touch him or help him down either until he gave her permission. "Seriously, can you move at all?"

He flexed his feet at the ankles and bent both knees slightly. Then Mac gave her a thumbs-up with his left hand. But she was right about his other arm. It trembled and he bit back a curse, but it refused to cooperate.

"Gloria at the hotel has called for an ambulance. Do you want to wait for them, or do you want me to help you down?" she asked.

"Down. Gently, please."

"And here I was planning to let you fall on your head," she grumbled.

The back door to the bar flew open and bounced off the scaffolding, shaking a yell out of Mac. "Sorry, buddy," a tall, dark-haired man said. "Are you okay?"

"I'm hanging upside down off your roof, Roy. Do I look okay?"

"I don't know who you are, but can you give me a hand?" Lori asked. The scaffolding itself looked solid as she ducked under a pipe to get closer to Mac. Unfortunately, she misjudged the distance and her shirt caught on the end of a bolt. There was a triangular tear in the middle of her bicep; no mending in the world would be able to hide the damage. "This was my favorite top."

"I'm sorry my rescue is inconveniencing you."

"So am I!"

The man grabbed Mac from the other side. Together, they braced his back as he swung one foot over a pipe, then pushed while Mac pulled himself into a somewhat seated position. From there, they held him steady as he slowly made his way to the ground.

Roy disappeared back into the bar for a moment and returned with a chair for Mac to sit on. "What happened?" he asked.

"Lightning strike," she and Mac said in harmony.

"That might be the first time we've ever agreed on anything," she said.

Mac tried to laugh, but it turned into a cough. "Oh, my ribs."

"I'm not surprised. Just sit still and stop yelling until you get checked out, will you?" Roy asked. Then he turned to her. "Did you call an ambulance?"

"Gloria at the Dew Drop Inn is calling for an ambulance and the fire department, since your roof is smoking."

"Thank you. I'm Roy, by the way. This is my bar."

"What are you thanking her for?" Mac asked. "Gloria made the call."

"What is wrong with you? I'm thanking her to be polite after she saved your ungrateful butt. You should be thanking her too, instead of being rude. It's not like this is her fault."

Lori liked this guy. "Thank you. My friends call me Lori."

Mac grimaced. His face had been bright red since hanging upside down had caused all the blood to run to his head. Now he was a lot paler than normal. "You don't know her like I do."

She would have insulted him back, but his lack of color and the sudden shakes he got were enough to make her grant him a little grace. If she'd narrowly escaped being hit by a bolt out of the blue, she might be a little snarky too. But that was his final assault. He settled into the chair and fell silent.

Lori sat with him quietly until the ambulance arrived. If he lost consciousness and hit the ground without her catching him, he'd never let her forget it. Roy showed the fire department the impact spot on the roof while she got Mac loaded into the ambulance. She stood awkwardly in the parking lot. Was there anything else she should be doing?

There wasn't. She'd done a good deed, and now she was done. After everything that had happened between her and Mac, and her and the town, helping him after an accident was a good way to end her relationship with Holiday Beach, especially since it was the second-to-last night she'd ever be in town.

CHAPTER 4

THERE WAS no way around it. Mac had to do it. He owed Lorelei Baker a thank-you for helping him the day before. He still wasn't entirely convinced she hadn't somehow arranged his accident, but he was pretty sure that was the painkillers talking.

It had taken forever to find a comfortable position to sleep in, and when he finally had, his pain medication had worn off, so he had to get out of bed, take another pill, and start all over in his nest of pillows and blankets. By the time he finally woke up, his alarm clock showed it was nearly noon. Doug had left him a message letting his brother know he'd bring over some lunch and they could decide how to handle this latest calamity in Mac's life.

When Mac messed up, he messed up huge. He couldn't have dislocated his shoulder at a worse time. Mackenzie Brothers Painting was booked solidly from May to October, especially when it came to painting exteriors. The Escape Room, where he'd had his accident, was the first of several businesses in Holiday Beach that were supposed to be given a fresh coat of paint and a facelift for the summer. With him out of the picture, the company's manpower was reduced by half.

Doug arrived with a pair of sandwiches and a bad attitude. "The good news is that we've had three locals call the office to apply for work," his younger, slightly taller brother said.

"That is good news."

"The bad news is we know all of them and don't want any of them."

"What about Caleb Quinn?" Mac asked. The teenager had been out of school for almost a year and had done odd jobs for them before.

"He's working full-time at By the Cup, but he's going to see what shifts he can give us. A few hours are better than none."

"Where are we going to find somebody this late in the season?" Any experienced college-aged painters were already working, and high school students still had more than a month of classes left to go. The company could lose a ton of contracts in the five weeks between now and then. Traditional recruiting would take time they didn't have.

Doug shrugged. "We could ask Lucy if she knows anybody. We might get lucky."

"How is it that she's been here for a year and knows more people than we do when we were born here?"

"Well, she's a lot prettier than you..."

His snort was the first time Mac had laughed all morning. "Fine. Talk to her."

"What are you going to be doing? Resting?"

"I have an errand to run first."

An hour later, he was wondering why he was wasting his time. All he wanted to do was say thank you to Lorelei

Baker, but he couldn't find her. She even made apologizing difficult. Gloria Vargas at the Dew Drop Inn said her guest was out and suggested he try looking for her at the Atlas Restaurant. Tripp Turner said she'd been in for lunch and mentioned checking out some of the shops on Richmond Road. She wasn't there either. He finally spotted her coming out of Flip Flop Fast and crossing the street, heading toward a bench overlooking the beach.

"Where have you been?" he demanded.

"What?"

"I've been looking all over for you."

"How could I possibly have known that?" Lorelei asked. Then she proceeded to ignore him in favor of her ice cream cone.

He huffed twice. On one hand, she was right; she couldn't have known he was looking for her. On the other hand, she could be a little nicer to a guy who was trying to say thank you.

"What did you need to see me about?" she asked, taking another lick of bright pink ice cream. "Because if it's about the Parkman build, I'm not responsible for that anymore."

"I'm trying to thank you for helping me yesterday."

She really looked at him for the first time. She took in the sling and the stiff way he held himself. "You're welcome. I hope they said you were going to have a fast recovery. I was concerned you'd broken more than your arm."

"I didn't break it. I dislocated my shoulder." He winced as he said it and was surprised when she did the same. "As for the rest, my ribs are battered and bruised, but not broken."

He'd done what he'd come to do. He didn't have to

say anything else to her. But now he needed to know. "Why isn't the Parkman project your responsibility anymore?" The disaster next door was nowhere near being done.

"They informed my boss they were dissatisfied with my work and, as a result, I was removed from the project. Unfortunately, there wasn't enough work to keep on a junior architect at the firm, so I was laid off."

He translated the calmly spoken statement in his head, and it was nothing he expected to hear. "You got fired?"

"I am now free to explore other opportunities."

She got fired. It hadn't even been her fault. Siggy had given him the rundown on who did what on his way home, telling Mac he'd left Mrs. Parkman yelling on her cell phone. "What are you doing back in Holiday Beach?" Mac asked. It wasn't like she had any friends in the area.

"Believe it or not, I won the grand prize of the Green, White, and Blue raffle. I bought tickets at By the Cup the last time I was in town. Since I don't have anywhere else to be, I figured I'd use my free nights at the Dew Drop Inn and do some online job hunting while enjoying the scenery."

"I suppose that's good luck," he said. "Anyway, thanks again."

Mac turned to go when she gently put her hand on his slinged arm. When he looked at her, she pointed at a well-muscled dog barrelling towards them, thirty pounds of brown fur and a slobbery smile with a leash flapping behind it. Racing in its wake was a harried Vietnamese lady in green leggings and a black T-shirt, screaming, "Barney, stop!"

Lori stepped in front of him and braced for impact if

the dog didn't change course. But it seemed intent on ignoring her and headed straight for the water. She raised one foot as the mutt ran by, focused on the narrow nylon leash, then slammed her foot down on it, bringing the dog to a sudden halt. She'd almost waited too long. The leash's retractable handle was only a foot from her shoe.

"Oh, thank you!" the jogger said. "Our obedience classes were going so well too. Bad, Barney." The dog dropped his head like he knew he'd been busted. He trotted to the woman's side and sat.

"Is he a swimmer, or does he just snap at the waves?" Lori asked.

"Barney's a swimmer. I can't convince him it's still too cold for a daily swim. Come June, he'll be in there every day. Thank you for saving me from an icy dip to get him. I'm Helen, by the way."

"No problem, Helen. I'm Lori."

Wow, Lori sounded like a friendly, regular person when she wasn't working. Who knew? "Hi, Helen. How are the girls?" he asked.

The black-haired woman crossed her eyes. "Hi, Mac. I'm taking a break before I try to come up with another argument for June as to why she can't paint her bedroom the colors she wants." She turned to Lori. "We're having my daughter's room repainted. I think I talked her out of pink lemonade. Now she's narrowed it down to either canary yellow or grape purple and I'm not sold on either," Helen told her.

"Teenager?"

"How'd you guess?"

Lori laughed. "I've painted a few bedrooms in my time. It was my summer job all the way through college. May I offer an idea?"

"Does it involve yellow or purple?"

Lori held her finger and thumb an inch apart. "A little bit. I'm not an interior designer, but have you considered a geometric design? You can find all kinds of very easy patterns online. You can paint something neutral on three of the walls, and then use purple, yellow, and white on the fourth wall. You could even add in the pink lemonade. She gets her colors, and you get to keep your eyesight."

Helen's brown eyes lit up. "That sounds ideal. It would really appeal to June's artistic side too. What do you think, Mac?"

"It's a little extra work, but it's not a bad idea," he admitted reluctantly. "Such small areas will keep the cost down since we won't be using much of each color of paint. Plus, one wall will be a lot easier to cover than all of them down the line. We can do that."

Barney gave a tug on his leash as he strained toward the lake again. "That's amazing news. Thanks again. I'm going to get this guy home and let June know what we decided." Helen waved as she resumed her run. The dog looked longingly over his shoulder before he started running beside her.

"I think you can let go of my arm now," Mac said.

She dropped it like it was fire. "No problem."

He couldn't figure out what to do next. He'd said thank you, which was all he had to do. But then she'd helped him, or rather helped Helen, figure out a problem that had stalled their job for weeks. Did he say thank you again? Or would Helen's thanks do? He didn't have the energy or brainpower to figure it out. "Thanks for the idea, Lorelei."

"You're welcome. And my friends and non-enemies call me Lori."

That was an olive branch he wasn't expecting. "Enjoy your mini vacation, Lori."

Pondering this new side of her, Mac wandered across the street to his favorite coffee shop. At this hour, with no rush of patrons stopping in for a cup of joe to get them to their jobs, the place was quiet. The bright wall of windows facing the beach let lots of sunshine flood the small coffee shop. The sidewalk tables were already filled, but there were only two occupied ones inside. Mac tossed his cap onto a free one, then limped to the counter.

"Did you get the number of that truck, Mac?"

He gave Rachel Best, the shop owner, a grin. "That good, huh?"

"Mac, I've seen roadkill with less bruises." She took his coffee order and handed him a mug and a wrapped dessert. "The cookie is on the house. It's not every day somebody I know gets up close and personal to a lightning bolt. It was shocking news, I tell you."

He groaned. "Is everybody going to make that joke?"

"All I know is I made it first. Be warned that Richie is going to ask you to hold a lightbulb to see if you can turn it on with the power of your mind." She waggled her fingers over her head as she said it, causing both of them to laugh.

"I'll consider myself warned." He spied an empty spot on the counter where a ticket book used to sit. "I think I ran into your fundraiser's winner."

"That Lori person. Yeah, she bought two tickets when she was in last week. Plus, she got Lucy's donated ticket."

"How did the fundraiser do?" he asked.

"Three thousand dollars," Rachel crowed. "We sold out. We'll have two dozen new garbage and recycling bins on the boardwalk and in the parks by the time our Memorial Day Weekend kicks off." The bell over the door tinkled and she darted back behind the counter. "Catch you next time."

He settled into the seat and saw Lori was still at the beach.

Of all the things she'd ever said to him, he couldn't get their last conversation out of his head, and he tried. Finally, he slid his phone out of his pocket. "Doug, where are you? I have a bad idea."

Half an hour later, he was still arguing.

"Are you sure you're not making a mistake, Bobby?" Although the question came from his little brother, in this case, it was also coming from his business partner. Mackenzie Brothers Painting was a two-man operation and had been since his brother graduated from high school. Robert and Doug Mackenzie were equal partners on paper. Mac was the face of the business and dealt with the clients; Doug handled the office work. They both wielded paintbrushes. This was a decision that had to be made together, but either way, it needed to be made.

"No, I'm not, which is why I want you to talk to her."

"You've done nothing but complain about Lorelei Baker for months."

Mac hadn't realized he'd been that vocal about her. But that was then, and this was now. "I know, but if we hired her, she'd be working for us instead of against us," he argued. He wished he could use a better argument, but the truth was they were stuck between a rock and a have-to-cancel-jobs place, and Lori was the only option they'd found. It was funny he didn't doubt her when she said she had experience. At any rate, it would be easy enough to check.

Doug was a little taller, a little thinner, and a little fairer than him, but there was no doubt they were brothers. They both looked like younger clones of their father, who was one of several Mackenzie male clones of the older generation. Which meant Mac recognized the stubborn look on his brother's face.

"Just talk to her," Mac said. "If you absolutely hate her, we'll start looking for somebody else. But don't hate her because I did." And because he wasn't above it, he wrapped his hand under the elbow in the sling and winced a bit to make himself look a little more pathetic.

"Fine, I'll talk to her," Doug muttered. "When's her interview?"

Now Mac winced for real. "Yeah. About that."

CHAPTER 5

LORI READ the email twice and still didn't understand it. She'd given Mac Mackenzie her phone number after the window incident to ensure there would be no further misunderstandings. Now that she was no longer working on the Parkman project, there was no reason for him to contact her. The words "Job Offer" in the subject line had to be part of some cruel joke.

It had been a beautiful afternoon to spend on the beach. She was surprised by how quiet it was. Then she realized school was still in session. The few kids there were under the supervision of their various grown-ups who seemed to be keeping one eye on the shoreline and the other on how much sand their charges were trying to eat.

There was no sign of the storm that had rolled over Holiday Beach the previous afternoon. Despite the clouds and the lightning, not a single drop of rain had fallen. The trees were full of bright green leaves and the hint of blossoms. Tulips and daffodils were in full bloom, paving the way for the small seedlings of marigolds and zinnias and other summer flowers recently added to the planters on the sidewalk. Holiday Beach was a pretty little town.

Lori finished the fruit kebob she'd purchased from Excalibur for a late-afternoon snack. Then she tried to find a garbage can near the food truck. A block later, she finally did. "Those new bins can't get here soon enough," she said to herself. Now she had the rest of the evening to herself. There were more interesting shops on Richmond Road that she hadn't checked out yet. Or she could head back to the inn, drag one of the lounge chairs by the pool into the sun, and work for an hour on her summer tan to cover her pasty stomach. Her options were endless since she had nowhere to be.

She chose the pool, which let her mull over Mac's strange communication in comfort. She wouldn't say he hated her, but he had no reason to call himself her friend. Why would he offer her a job with their history and the animosity between them? It had to be a joke. A mean one, considering it was the only offer she'd received.

Then he sent a second email with the subject line, "Are you still in town?"

"Why?" she sent back.

"Because I'm serious about the job."

Twenty minutes later, she was parked on his gravel driveway. Mac was on his front porch with another man. There was a third lawn chair, empty, on the deck. It was as good a place as any to have an impromptu interview.

His brother, Doug, started with the big question. "Why aren't you working for the Parkmans anymore? Did they fire you because of the ways you messed up with Mac?"

She hesitated before she answered. "That was part of it."

"Why haven't you got another job yet?" Doug pressed.

"In the week since I lost the last one? I'm an excellent architect, Mr. Mackenzie, but I'm not that good. I've let my network know I'm looking for new opportunities. I haven't had any offers yet, but it's early days," she said. It was all true at the moment, but she'd probably have the same answer a week or a month from now.

"Why did you come there today?"

"Because Mac said he was offering me a job and I have bills to pay. I admit it's really weird he called me because we are so not friends, but I'm in no position to turn down work." Pride only took a person so far; student loans took them a lot further.

Doug shrugged. "Fair enough. Bob says you have painting experience. What's worse? Trim work or taping?"

She made a face. "Both are the un-fun parts of the job, but if I had to pick one, I'd say trim work. At least with taping, you have the pleasure of ripping it all off at the end."

Doug smiled for the first time. "I'd say taping."

Mac leaned forward and spoke for the first time. "Would you actually work for us?"

"Painting? Yes. Although as I said, I don't know why you called me of all people."

"I'm out of play for the next month or so and we need another experience painter ASAP."

"And I'm your first pick?"

He laughed. "You're our only option," he corrected.

"Ouch," she said. The truth hurt. But at least they

were being honest. "I would. Because you're my only option right now as well."

"It'll only be a short-term contract until I can get back to work," Mac said.

"I can work around that. What if I get a better offer before you're ready to come back?"

"We'd appreciate as much notice as you could give us."

It was the weirdest and shortest interview she'd ever had. It was also the most desperate she'd ever been. She already had two bills sitting in her inbox. "Let's talk turkey. Do I get a company hat?"

By the time Lori returned to the hotel, she had an official job offer waiting in her inbox. It wasn't one she wanted, but it was one she needed. Her only concern was her lack of a place to stay. It was pointless to take the job if she had to spend her entire paycheck on a hotel room.

She'd just settled on her bed with a takeout margherita pizza and a classic animated movie on the television when the phone rang. The hotel room's phone, not her personal cell. "Lori, it's Gloria at the front desk. I have a call that's asking to be put through to you. It's Lucy Callahan."

"I don't know a Lucy Callahan."

"She manages the Remington Arms apartments in town. She said Mac asked her to call you?"

The hotel manager sounded as confused as she felt. "Sure. Please put the call through." Lori wiped her hands on a napkin and sat a little straighter, even though nobody else could see her. When the phone rang again, she answered with a professional, "Hello, this is Lori."

"Hi. We haven't met. My name is Lucy. Bob and Doug Mackenzie asked me to give you a call. I understand you're looking for a short-term rental in town. There are tons of bed-and-breakfast vacation rentals in the area if you're looking for one of those. But if you're looking for your own place, I have a very small apartment that might fit the bill if you're interested."

"I might be if the price is right."

"It's a studio unit in one of my buildings. I usually don't do short-term rentals, but I'm looking for somebody who might be willing to paint and do some work for a discount on the rent. Mac suggested I talk to you."

Lori went silent for a moment. Her pride could only take so many hits before she wanted to cry. Having to live in a fixer-upper apartment while she worked for a guy who vocally didn't like her was rock bottom. If things got any worse, she'd have to change her name and move to another state.

The woman at the other end of the call read her silence for what it was. "There's no pressure. If you'd like to see the apartment, you're welcome to come to the Remington Arms any time tomorrow before noon. I'll be here all morning and be happy to show it to you. If you're not interested, it's fine. I thought it was strange luck we had one unit left, but it may be meant for somebody else."

"Strange luck," Lori echoed. A memory popped into her head. "Your name is Lucy?"

"Yes."

"Did you buy a raffle ticket at By the Cup and leave it for the next person to have?"

"Yes. Are you...?"

"You're the reason I'm in Holiday Beach this weekend! Thanks for the ticket. It worked." Suddenly, the almost insulting offer seemed like a genuine opportunity.

"I have to be out of the hotel at eleven tomorrow morning. Can I come over after that to see the place?"

"That sounds good. I'll see you then."

Lori settled into the pillows and chose the largest slice of pizza in the box. Pizza and pop, a comfy nest and a good movie, a job and a potential apartment. Her streak of bad luck might finally be ending.

CHAPTER 6

SHE WAS PROMPT. Early even. It was a good start. She was also dressed to work in sneakers and clean jeans, although they were frayed a little around the cuffs, and a collared T-shirt in the same navy blue as the Mackenzie Brothers Painting logo. Lori smiled hesitantly when she saw him. "Good morning, Mac."

"Morning, Lori. Are you all settled in?"

"Pretty much."

According to local gossip, she'd had quite the weekend. Lucy told her boyfriend Roy, who told him Lori had signed a one-month lease on a studio unit in an apartment block Lucy managed. She'd driven back to Minneapolis on Sunday afternoon and returned with a pickup full of furniture. That evening, she'd returned to the city and made the trip one more time with her own car full of clothes and smaller items. That was a lot of driving for a month's work. If nothing else, it let him know she was serious.

Unfortunately, they were throwing her into the deep end on her first job. It was supposed to be him and Doug working on the old Holiday House, a sprawling, two-story mansion with a ton of windows and gingerbread. It was a monster of a project that would be at least a week of long days. "Welcome to Mackenzie Brothers Painting," he said, waving his hand at the project.

She gulped. He didn't laugh. He did smile, though, when he pulled a ball cap from behind his back. "You're on the team."

Lori gave him another small smile. "You're all heart." She nodded at the house. "Are we doing the inside or the outside?"

"Outside, for now."

She looked at the sky, and it was another clear, beautiful May morning. "I checked the forecast. We're in for a perfect week."

"Let's get you set up."

With a job this big, he and Doug had already decided on a plan of attack. The three of them circled the property and he pointed out areas of special attention. Then the clock hit eight, and Mac left them to it.

Half an hour later, he was sitting in the office with a fresh coffee from By the Cup, already bored out of his mind. He couldn't be on-site. He'd offer more problems than help. The frustration was half of his problem.

The other half was nerves that he'd made a terrible mistake in offering the job to Lori. It was a little late, but he had checked her references. He called the number she gave him as soon as the office opened. The owner had nothing but good things to say about the four summers she'd painted for them. It was the compliments that had him worried: innovative thinker, goal oriented, problem solver. She probably had half a dozen ideas for improvements and was haranguing Doug about better ways to do things when they already had a long-time system that worked. How could he have left her alone with his poor, defenseless baby brother?

Mac left the coffee on his desk and jumped back into the truck to ride to the rescue.

It was all for nothing. By the time he arrived at the Holiday House, an hour after he left, the one set of attic windows was already covered with paper, and Lori was at the top of a ladder with a paint scraper. She waved at him, then got right back to work.

"What happened?" Mac asked his brother.

"I told her what needed to be done. She asked for help with the ladder, got into the safety harness, and got to work. She's a machine."

"It's only been an hour."

"A productive hour," Doug argued.

"Any problems so far?"

"A profound schism in our musical tastes when it comes to the radio, but she has her phone and earbuds. We're fine. Why are you back here?"

He'd sound like a real jerk if he said he was expecting Lori to cause problems. "I got bored at the office already," Mac said. That way, he was only a familial jerk for wasting his brother's time.

Doug sighed. "I was expecting this."

Now he was insulted. "What?"

"You don't do well with inactivity, big bro. I love you, but it's going to be a long month if you can't find a way to keep yourself occupied." To Mac's shock, Doug pulled a folded sheet of paper from his pants pocket. "I jotted down some ideas of things you can do in the office for me since I'm going to be spending more time than usual on the jobsite. If you're up to it." Doug lifted an eyebrow, as if daring Mac to decline his offer.

Mac grabbed the list and held it to his forehead like a salute. "Yes, boss. I'm off."

He returned to his truck but didn't start it right way. The windows were down, and the day was nice enough he didn't need the heater or the air conditioner. Doug's to-do list took the whole page. Mac was grateful to see it wasn't all busy projects to keep him out of his little brother's hair. All the tasks were directly related to upcoming jobs and would save them time in the long run.

He started with an easy one: getting the paint for the Pham project. They were painting both girls' rooms. Now that June's colors had been decided, he could buy the paint they needed and have it boxed and ready to go for when Doug finished the Holiday job.

Handler Hardware was bustling. The little indie store that could had survived for decades, and local support meant that when a big-box store had tried to open between Holiday Beach and Bixby, the community had argued the short-term price gains weren't worth the long-term effect on the economy when it took the place of a dozen shops in the area. They'd been proven right, too, when the large Farmerville store in the next county over closed its doors a decade after driving all the local businesses under. Now a new generation was running the store.

"Hey, Mac. Electrifying news." The tall blonde behind the counter grinned.

"Not you too, Julie," he groaned good-naturedly.

"You have to give us at least a month of puns," she said.

"Two days," he bargained.

"A week. Final offer." She stuck her hand across the counter, and he shook it to seal the deal. "Now, what can I do for you? We have some paint rollers on sale. The price will shock you."

"It's going to be a long week," he muttered. But that was the last joke she made before they got down to business. Julie Handler had taken the store over from her parents a few years prior and had nearly everything a contractor needed, including a full selection of paints, stains, and finishes. When he explained why he only needed the smallest cans of paint, she nodded in surprise at the bold yet not overwhelming design.

Then he told her who'd suggested it.

Her happy, teasing mood evaporated. "Oh. Is she back?"

Mac had been in the store when Lori had tried to pressure Julie into giving her a massive discount on her purchases. The out-of-towner had not made a good impression, and apparently it had lingered. "Lori isn't on the Parkman project anymore. She's on a short-term contract with Mackenzie Brothers. She seems to be a lot more personable now that she's no longer working over there." Julie's blank face and sharp eyes didn't soften at that news. "But I'll be the one picking up our orders for the next little while, anyway. It's one of the few things I can do." He tapped his sling, and her smile returned a bit.

"Seriously, I'm glad it wasn't more serious than that. It must have been scary," Julie said. "You were lucky Roy got to you so quickly."

The bartender had helped, but Mac was obligated to give credit where it was due. It might help temper Lori's initial impression as well. "He was great, but Lori was actually the first person on the scene. She saw the lightning strike and was over and helping before I even knew what had happened. I owe her one."

"Is that why you gave her a job?"

"It's part of it," he admitted. "She started today, and Doug seems happy with her work."

Julie scoffed. "We'll see how long that lasts."

Mac shrugged his good shoulder. He wasn't about to change her mind in a single morning. In fact, he'd already done more than he had to. "I'll let you make another joke if you help me load all of this into the car." He gestured at his full cart.

"Fine. But we still have to ring you up. Not that I think you're going to bolt without paying."

He groaned again. "Such a long week."

CHAPTER 7

In a few days, Lori would be proud of the work she'd accomplished. Right now, she was too tired and sore to care. Spending all day outside in the sun balancing on a ladder with her arms over her head while scraping paint had left her a quivering wreck.

The brand-new tub and shower liner looked pretty as she stood under the hot spray, trying to work up the energy to rub some conditioner into her hair. She finally managed to squirt a bit into her palm and massage it in before she needed another break. She used the time to study the bathroom.

Like the rest of the one-room apartment, it needed a fresh coat of paint. The towel bar hung crookedly, and the plastic silver veneer was peeling. Lori made a note to replace it when she patched the wall. The ceiling was stained with nicotine she imagined was decades old. It had been years since anyone was allowed to smoke in a rented apartment, although more than one person had likely cheated in the bathroom with the fan running. Fixing that was going to take a few coats of paint. She couldn't fix the worn linoleum or the battered vanity, but those weren't her problem. All she had to do was patch and paint.

The main room wasn't much better. The floor matched the bathroom. The patches in front of the stove and sink in the kitchen area were so worn that none of the original color was left. A poorly done paint job showed an older baby blue under the current sand brown when she looked at the electrical outlets and around the window trim. She'd do a better job.

But not tonight.

Doug had called it a day at five and thanked her for her work. She could tell he meant it and was impressed by their progress. He'd also let her know the next day they'd be working at ground level to give themselves a break, but they'd be back on the ladders on Wednesday to finish the middle section. Painting would be the fastest and easiest part of the job.

She set the alarm on her phone, as well as the one on the clock of her charging port. She had wisely eaten before her shower, so all she had to do was fall into bed, even though it was only eight o'clock and the sun was still high in the sky. The skinny futon mattress wasn't like sleeping on a cloud. But she had clean sheets, a warm blanket, and a dark room once the curtains were pulled.

Lori didn't even remember closing her eyes.

She opened them three minutes before her alarm was set to go off. She'd wisely given herself an extra half hour to get ready. After a solid ten minutes of stretching, Lori was loose enough to complete a set of Tai Chi. By the time she finished the last of the hundred and eight moves, she was centered and ready to meet the day. She ate a solid breakfast, packed a lunch in her cooler, and set off for another day of hard work.

Mac was on-site again by the time she arrived. She didn't know why, unless he expected her not to show. But that couldn't be it because he had three coffees and offered one to her. "Good morning. I have milk and sugar packets, but this is straight black," he said in greeting.

"Morning, and thanks! Please pass the sugar."

"I don't see any ladders yet. What's the game plan?" he asked.

"We're starting from ground level today and going as high as we can sand and scrape. Tomorrow we'll do what's left in the middle and start taping and preparing to paint," she told him as she struggled to get the lid off without burning herself.

"We always work from the top down. Doug knows that," Mac said. His voice was sharp, and he looked annoyed. At her. Even though she hadn't done anything.

Was this how it was going to be? Blaming her for anything that went wrong, whether it was her fault or not. She might as well be working for the Parkmans again. "It was his idea."

"It was," Doug agreed. "All the intricate preparation on the trim and second floor was freaking hard work. You and I miscalculated trying to do it on ladders. That gingerbread is killer. We need to give ourselves a day to recover before we go back up there."

"Okay," Mac agreed, like he hadn't accused her of stomping all over the Mackenzie Brothers Painting procedure like an unwelcome elephant.

Lori shouldn't be surprised. Her reputation was fairly based on her actions at her last job. But this was only her second day. It was going to be a long month if her past was thrown in her face every time she did or said something Mac didn't like.

But the sooner she proved him wrong, the happier she'd be. "Doug, I'll get the gear out of the van. Thanks again for the coffee, Mac."

As she hurried away, there was a slap of a hand hitting skin. "What was that?" Doug whispered.

She didn't stick around to hear the rest of the conversation.

Lori had slightly more pep at the end of her second day. She assumed it was the energy she hadn't expended climbing up and down ladders a hundred times. Mac had left after dropping off the coffees, and she and Doug had worked in silence until he broached a conversation about the weather. That broke the ice Mac's frostiness had caused, and they spent the rest of the day in friendly chatter.

Now, rather than return to her nice but tiny room and spend another evening in near isolation, she decided to enjoy the resort town. Starting with the cool-looking bar next to the hotel where she'd stayed.

The Escape Room was a tiki bar in northern Minnesota, which was novel enough. The patio lanterns strung around the thatch-covered portico set the tone immediately. The Hawaiian-themed shirts the staff wore only reinforced it. Lori took in the clock that hung between the flags of various Caribbean countries. Although every hour was marked with a "5," it was actually after five o'clock here, not just in some random somewhere.

Despite the empty stools along the bar, a woman took the seat right next to her. Lori looked over to see a familiar face. The black-haired woman was still wearing her nametag. "Hi, Gloria. Good to see you again," Lori said.

The Dew Drop Inn's assistant manager smiled. "Hi. I see you've found the best watering hole in Holiday Beach." The waitress behind the counter pulled each of them a beer and quickly moved on to the next customers who were coming in to celebrate the end of their work-days. "What brings you back to town? I didn't think we'd see you again after your contest win."

"I got a temp job in town when I really needed one. This is only a pit stop."

"I hope you enjoy your time here. The beginning of summer is the best."

"Are you speaking from experience? Are you from Holiday Beach?" Lori asked.

"No. Vargas isn't generally a family name that's been around for generations in these parts. I ended up here the same way you did," Gloria said. "I was working in San Antonio when I took a short-term assignment here as the assistant manager of the Dew Drop Inn. That was back when it was part of the Longfellow hotel chain. Manage-ment changed, I got promoted, and I've been in Holiday Beach for about a year and a half now."

"How do you like it?"

"I've just survived my second Minnesota winter, so it's safe to say I like it a lot. It's very different from the San Antonio winters I'm used to."

"I'm guessing frostbite isn't a problem in south Texas?"

Gloria's brown eyes sparkled with laughter. "Not usually, no."

A tall, dark-haired man stopped to talk to them. To Lori's surprise, she recognized him too. "Roy, right?"

"You bet. You're Mac's knight in shining armor." He stuck out his hand. "We were never properly introduced. Roy Wagner. This is my place."

"It's fun. Good beer," she complimented.

"Thanks again for helping Mac. He scared ten years off my life when I went around back and found him dangling off the scaffolding—"

"Like a fish on a hook," they finished together.

It had been horrifying at the time, but Roy seemed to share her dark humor. "I think Mac's doing better now, despite his shoulder. I saw him this morning and he was moving pretty well. Doug says he's going a little squirrelly in the office, though."

"I don't doubt it. He's an active guy. He's probably not happy about the delay when it comes to working on his house, but he'll get it done, eventually. I'm just glad he's okay."

This was nice. Apparently not everybody in Holiday Beach hated her. Okay, it was only the people she hadn't dealt with on the Parkman project, but she did have a few folks who might be glad to see her.

Gloria and the bartender, Emily, started talking to her about the season finale of *Santa Monica, E.R*, which meant Lori had to vigorously defend Chris Carmichael's hotness against that of Cameron Irvine. Then Lucy arrived, kissed her fiancé, and threw Danny DaSilva into the competition. Lori spent the next hour truly enjoying herself in Holiday Beach for the first time.

CHAPTER 8

SATURDAY MORNING HAD TAKEN FOREVER to arrive. Not only had Mac caught up on all his paperwork, but he had also finished most of Doug's. When he was done with that, he went online and started leaving reviews for all the suppliers and contractors they worked with. He completed all of those by the end of business on Thursday.

On Friday, he took it upon himself to shred old documents. One page at a time. That wasted two hours. He didn't know if he'd survive another month of being useless.

Now somebody was interrupting the time he actually wanted to be lazy. It took a moment to realize the hammering was someone pounding on his front door and not a bird going to town on a tree outside his window. Mac stumbled down the stairs and threw open the door, half expecting it to be Lori Baker letting him know of another catastrophe she'd caused on his property.

He was half right. Lori was the one who got him out of bed.

But he didn't know who was more shocked—him or her.

Her jaw hit the floor when she saw him standing there in all his glory in his old cutoff shorts and with a full-blown case of bedhead. "What?" he barked.

"It's eight o'clock?" she squeaked. Her hand shook so hard coffee sloshed out of the cup she held. She winced when the hot liquid spilled over her fingers.

"Well, come in and stop burning yourself," he ordered. "Bathroom's the first door on the right under the stairs."

What was she doing here? It was Saturday. Did she think they worked on weekends? Didn't Doug tell her he'd see her on Monday? Or did she think it was her job to make his life miserable every single day she was in Holiday Beach?

She was off to a good start.

Okay, so she'd been on time on Monday. And Tuesday. And for the rest of the week. But her very presence had him checking in with his brother every hour on the hour for the first couple of days until Doug threatened to tie him to a lightning rod to finish the job if he didn't leave them in peace. On Wednesday, he cruised past the Holiday House after Lori and Doug had left for the day, just to see if they were on schedule. They had been, but he'd spotted some very shoddy patches where somebody hadn't done a proper job of scraping the trim.

Mac grimaced at the memory of when he went back on Thursday morning to let Doug know... He thought he was being thoughtful when he pulled his brother aside to complain about the quality of Lori's work, only to discover that not only was it Doug's patch, but he'd had to stop halfway through the job in that area and intended to finish that morning.

"Listen, Bobby, if you're uncomfortable with her working for us, say so. She's still in her trial period, so it's no harm, no foul. But if you don't want to fire her, you have to stop this nitpicking. Lori's doing a good job. She's fast and efficient. She's good to work with. We're a little behind where you and I would be, but she and I haven't had time to develop the same dynamic. You have a history with her, but she was doing her job. Accidents happened. You need to make up your mind and stop looking for reasons to get rid of her." What made it worse was Doug wasn't mad at him.

He was disappointed in his big brother.

Thursday had been a quiet day of really thinking about what he wanted to do. His decision came just before he closed the office for the day. Helen Pham had sent an email.

"June LOVES the geometric design idea. Attaching the pattern we want for the full wall. She almost changed her mind on colors, but confirm original Real Raisin, Electric Canary, and Strawberry Lemonade colors we discussed, and something neutral and white/cream for the rest of the walls. Let me know when you can start."

It was a sign. He made one more drive to Holiday House the next afternoon. Doug and Lori were loading the van. The house was done; two stories of gleaming white beauty. It looked spectacular. It would be the envy of every homeowner on Star Lake. Determined to start on the right foot, that's what he led with.

Doug gave him a small smile. Lori beamed. "Thank you. She was a lot of work, but she really is a beauty. I've been checking out the neighborhood as I've been driving to work in the morning. No other house in the area can match the gingerbread."

"It's a great job, Lori. We handed you a monster out of the gate, but you delivered."

He didn't think she could smile any harder, but she did. "Thank you."

"Can I take the two of you out for a beer to celebrate the end of your first week?" he asked.

"I'd really like to say yes, but I made plans with Gloria and Emily to go out for an early supper." She sounded sincere.

"I'll say yes to a beer, Bobby." Now Doug was grinning like there was no tomorrow and he was stuck taking his brother out for a drink.

"Fine. Meet me at the Escape Room once you've cleaned up. Lori, have a good weekend," he said.

He'd ended the week on a very friendly note. He had no idea why she was waking him up at the crack of eight on the weekend. Was she trying to ruin his life? What other explanation could there be when he was being so nice?

When she came out of the bathroom, he gave her a good look. He recognized her paint-spattered tennis shoes that had originally been blue. Instead of a neutral T-shirt, hers said "Hit Hard, Run Fast, Turn Left" over a pair of crossed baseball bats. Her jean shorts had rolled up hems and revealed calves too pink to be natural; she needed to use more powerful sunscreen if she was going to be working outside over the summer. She wasn't dressed for work, so why was she at his house? "You do know you have Saturdays off, don't you?"

"Yes."

"So why are you in my living room?" he demanded.

At the sound of tires crunching on gravel, he raised a hand to cut off her answer. Mac moved to the window as his brother's van and three other familiar vehicles pulled into his long driveway. Doug, Roy, Caleb, and Josh Huntington from the town's most popular gym all trudged to the house.

"What is happening?" he asked, not expecting an answer.

"We're here to work. I thought you knew," she replied.

Doug looked at the window and waved. Then he led the other men into the house without pausing to knock. His brother stared at him. "Why aren't you ready?"

"For a home invasion?" Doug's shocked expression looked like it matched the one he was wearing. Mac raised his good hand. "What?"

"We discussed this. Last night at the bar. About you falling behind on the house and having to get the drywall done," Doug prompted.

"Yes. And?" A headache was coming on. His arm had ached all night long, only giving him an hour of uninterrupted sleep at a time.

Roy laid his hand on Mac's good shoulder as he walked past him and headed into the living room. Josh gave him a friendly wave and followed Roy.

"I told you a bunch of us felt bad you were stressing out about it."

"I know," Mac said, rubbing his temples.

"Did you miss the part where I said we were coming over to install the drywall on the main floor so we could start priming?"

"Apparently." Mac glanced over his shoulder. The guys were already getting organized, pulling tools off the top of the stack of material in the middle of the living room and looking for electrical outlets to plug in battery chargers for the saws and drills. "I guess I need pants."

"I'm sure Lori will appreciate it."

"Why is she even here?"

"Because we—meaning you—need the help, and I told her if she lent a hand, she could have the half-empty containers of filler from the storage room and some sandpaper to prime the walls of her apartment. She promised Lucy she'd paint them as part of her rent," Doug explained.

It wasn't totally altruistic, but she also didn't have to help at all. "Hey, everybody," Mac said, raising his voice. "I missed the part where you were coming over, but I appreciate it. Give me a couple of minutes to get dressed and then I'll start bossing you around since I'm pretty much useless beyond that. I'm grateful you all came today."

"You could always make a donut run to Butterlicious to show your appreciation," Caleb said. The twenty-year-old had come a long way in the last six months. The once-homeless teen now had a small apartment, a full-time job as a barista at By the Cup, and still worked a few hours for Mackenzie Brothers Painting. It meant a lot to Mac that the young man had given up one of the few days he had off in order to help him.

"I can do that," Mac said. He took orders from the guys, then got to Lori.

"Anything with jelly, please."

"Those are my favorite too." He smiled, and when she returned it, it felt they had something in common they didn't have to work at for the first time.

By the time he got out of the shower, they had two

sheets up. Doug and Josh were holding a third while Caleb held it in place, and Roy was marking and cutting a fourth. Lori stood over a pail, mixing a batch of plaster. He would have to spring for a full dozen at the rate they were working.

By the time he returned, the guys had finished an entire wall, including cutting out the holes for the electrical fixtures. Lori was mudding the cracks, daubing plaster on paper to tack it into place and then applying an even coat to seamlessly blend the various boards into a smooth wall. "Need a hand?" he asked. "I can hold the tape while you mud." It was a one-handed job.

"Absolutely."

Slather, scrape, repeat. "You're good at this," Mac noted. She wasn't cracking jokes like the other guys, but her job required a little more concentration.

"Thanks. My maternal grandpa was a drywaller. He's the reason I got interested in house construction." There was nothing but respect in her blue eyes when she said, "He was the one who taught me to paint too. If it can be done to a wall or ceiling, I'm pretty sure I've seen it done, if not helped do it myself."

"Installed tin ceiling tiles?" he asked.

Lori flinched. "I feel so bad about that. I ordered them through Handler Hardware to try and give some business to a local store and Julie Handler had to make a special order. Then Mrs. Parkman changed her mind at the last minute. Again. Julie couldn't return them. She took such a hit. I hope she can find another buyer for them."

Mac wanted to kick his own butt. He knew Julie was bitter about the return, but it sounded like Lori felt even worse. "Unfortunately, they aren't going to work with my interior design, otherwise I'd buy them myself. They are beautiful."

"Do you know which house they would suit? The Holiday House. I saw their kitchen through the window. They'd fit the tone of the house perfectly."

"They would." He'd taken a tour of the house when they'd given the quote to paint it. Even the upgrades were designed to keep the early-twentieth-century aesthetic. Mac had orders to paint the kitchen ceiling, but he made the instant decision to mention the tin tiles to the owner as an alternative. It would make him look good and get Julie out of a tight spot with surplus, unmoveable inventory. If he mentioned Lori, the woman who'd accidentally caused the problem, had also provided the solution, it might help in mending fences.

They called it a day late in the afternoon, after he'd made another run to grab a couple of pizzas for his crew to share. It had been a small price to pay. By the time they were done, the six of them had managed to finish drywalling the downstairs bedroom, including the large closet. Not only that, but they had also made it all the way around most of the massive open concept living room, dining room, and kitchen on the main floor. All that was missing was the area behind the woodstove, which needed to be installed in the corner. It was on the way to being a home.

And Lori was on her way to being a real person in his world, not the bogeyman who used to work next door. Mac was surprised. It turned out when you spend four solid hours working with somebody rather than fighting with them, you could discover you had a lot in common.

They'd both stuck to neutral topics, but once he found out Lori was also a Twins fan, the morning had flown by as they talked about the team's chances for the season.

"I'm buying everyone a round at the Escape Room. Are you coming?"

"Thanks, but I really have to go. I have four weekends to get the apartment painted, and with what Doug gave me, I can get the bathroom done this weekend." Lori looked around from the center of the main floor of his house. From her position, she could see the living room, the dining area, the kitchen, and the stairs leading to the second floor. Behind the newly drywalled wall in the living room was the newly done main floor bedroom and the bathroom, the only completely finished room in the house. "I hadn't seen the inside of your place before. It's going to be fantastic."

"Thanks for helping get it this far," he said, meaning it.

"On the inside, at least."

He widened his eyes at her joke.

"I'll see you on Monday at the office," Lori said before she waved to the others and slipped out the front door.

"Didn't she want to stick around?" Josh asked. The gym owner had managed to stay spotless throughout the entire morning. As far as Mac knew, he was the only person there who hadn't met Lori before. He was asking about her with a little too much interest to just be friendly.

"She had plans," Mac said.

"Maybe I should offer her some free passes to Diesel Fitness. She's new to Holiday Beach. It would be a good way for her to meet people," Josh continued.

"I don't know if she's going to be here that long." Which was a shame. She was a good fit for his hometown.

CHAPTER 9

LORI STOOD at her counter eating pizza out of the box and drinking water from a glass covered with paint-smudged fingerprints. She was going to miss Colombo's when she left Holiday Beach. It had the best margherita pizza she'd ever had in her life.

Or maybe she was hungrier than she'd ever been in her life. That could be it too. Seven hours of mudding and taping at Mac's house, followed by another four hours of patching and sanding her bathroom walls and painting the bathroom ceiling had her muscles begging for mercy.

But it had been a good day.

She'd spent the day with Mac Mackenzie and come away unscathed after her unexpected arrival. He was a decent human when she wasn't making his life a misery. She could like him. If he wasn't her boss. His friends weren't bad either.

She might like Mac, but she was head over heels in love with his house. It was nothing like anything she'd designed. It was much too traditional for the clients who came to her old company wanting something "contemporary," "abstract" or "ground-breaking." Heaven forbid they have a setup that wasn't unique.

Lori didn't think there was anything wrong with traditional. Mac had chosen an open plan for the main floor. She didn't know what he wanted to do with the staircase, but she had ideas that would keep the aesthetic uncluttered. She hadn't asked him or offered any suggestions. One morning without an argument did not make them best friends. Besides, all she'd seen were the bones. She had no idea what his tastes were.

She polished off a fourth slice and put the rest in the fridge for Sunday's supper. If she'd timed it correctly, her bathroom was now at the barely dry stage. It wouldn't withstand the long, hot shower her aching body craved, but it could handle a cool bath where she could scrub off the plaster and paint she'd managed to coat her arms and legs with.

As she climbed into bed before the sun went down again, noises floated up the street from the beach that was blocks and blocks away. It sounded like a good time. Unfortunately, she wasn't used to physical labor anymore, and six days in a row turned out to be her limit. She promised herself she'd finish the bathroom in the morning and then give herself the rest of Sunday off to relax before starting all over the next day.

Lori awoke free of aching shoulders and burning quads. She put her phone on the vanity and set her favorite beach-inspired playlist at a volume that was loud but not overpowering as she went to work. She was just finishing when there was a knock at her apartment door.

Lucy, her landlord and vacation-ticket provider, shifted from foot to foot. Her sandy-blonde hair was pushed off her forehead with a thin black headband. "I was wondering if..." She sniffed. "If you'd had a chance to plan what you want to do, but I smell paint. Have you started already?"

Lori stepped aside and gestured at the bathroom. Lucy grinned when she saw it. "This is fantastic. The walls look great. We'll get you a new towel bar and toilet-paper holder."

"There's enough paint left to do a little trim work if you replace the vanity. I painted behind the toilet tank as far as I could reach, but I couldn't do the whole thing," Lori told her.

Lucy waved away her words. "It looks great." Then she looked at Lori. "Tell me you're not working on a Sunday."

"I was, but I was done for the day. Unless you wanted me to do the main room right away." She hoped that wasn't the case. The weather forecast said it was going to be a gorgeous afternoon. She wanted to explore more of the town.

"No, I want you to get outside and relax. Or be inside and relax. Roy told me you helped at Mac's yesterday. You should take it easy today."

"Wow, there really are no secrets in a small town."

Lucy laughed. "We manage to keep one or two under wraps. But if you do happen to go to the beach, you might want to be there around noon. In case there's an unscheduled, supposedly secret announcement being made or something."

A day on the beach was exactly what she needed. "I'll be there. Totally coincidentally, of course."

Lucy's suggestion was perfect. Lori found a spot on the edge of the sandy beach that was in full sun but shielded from the wind. More brave kids splashed around in the water than the previous weekend, but only a couple dunked themselves fully. They screeched the moment they surfaced, then raced back to their towels and parents who showered them with I-told-you-sos.

A couple of minutes after twelve, speakers attached to the whitewashed gazebo at the top of the park crackled to life. "Attention, beachgoers and volunteers. The Holiday Beach Parks Committee is going to be out in full force today installing twenty-four garbage and recycling bins along the beach, greenspace, and parks around town. Please use them and encourage others to as well, so we can keep Holiday Beach and Star Lake looking fantastic this summer."

Lori didn't recognize the voice speaking, but she did see a familiar face. Rachel from the coffee shop was one of a pair pulling a set of blue and black bins through the sand toward a lifeguard tower. Her companion was a tall, blond man being led by a little boy who could barely keep himself upright as he trudged through the sand, pulling one of the man's hands.

She got up to assist. After her hunt for a garbage can the previous weekend, she knew how badly they were needed. "These are going to be really helpful. How busy does the beach get in the summer?" she asked.

Rachel twisted the bin to settle it solidly in the sand. "It'll be packed every day from Memorial Day weekend to Labor Day. We got these just under the wire."

"Let me be the first to put it to use." Lori tossed her water bottle into the recycling bin, purposely bouncing it off the sides to make a loud noise.

"Dad, she used it already!"

"You bet. I was looking for a recycling bin last weekend. Thanks for bringing this one to the beach," Lori said to the little cutie.

"Lori, this is my boyfriend Owen and his son Richie. Guys, this is Lori. She bought tickets to raise money for the garbage bins and was the winner."

Owen smiled at her. "Thanks for keeping Holiday Beach clean." Then he turned to his son. "We're off to the races, buddy. Are you ready to deliver another set of bins?"

"And then ice cream?" the little boy bargained.

"And then lunch," Rachel countered. It sounded like a familiar argument.

"Fine."

Rachel, Owen, and Richie drew more people who wanted to talk to them. All the new people on the beach surrounded her old quiet spot, turning it into a hive of activity. Not wanting to sit in the noise and not ready to go home, Lori headed for the docks she saw in the distance. It was a lovely walk along the road between the beach and the marina, with a rocky patch of shoreline separating the two.

A small wooden building on the road's edge announced it was the Pollux Gas Station. A single gas pump sat at the edge of the shoreline, with the Castor Marina docks just below it. It wasn't busy now, but Lori could imagine a long row of bobbing boats waiting for their turns to fill their tanks.

She spied a large, fenced parking lot on the other side of the road, stuffed with tarp-covered boats on trailers. That made sense. When she looked at the marina, most of the slips were still open, with only a few boats already in the water. One of the open fishing boats had a figure standing in it, awkwardly yanking on a cord and trying to coax an outboard motor to life.

"Mac?" she called. She didn't know he had a boat. That shouldn't be surprising. She didn't know much about him at all. But she didn't spot any fishing gear lying in the boat, which made his urgency weird.

"Lori? Help me!" He stumbled away from the engine, his shirt already stained with sweat.

"What's wrong?" she asked as she hurried down the unstable floating deck.

He used his good hand to point up the shoreline. Past the beach and the marina and heading for the middle of the lake was a small rubber air mattress with a tiny body on it. Nobody else had noticed it yet.

"Show me what to do and then stand back," she ordered.

It was the choke that caused all her problems. She yanked the cord, but despite all the sputtering, the engine refused to turn over. It turned into a two-person job as she yanked the cord and Mac adjusted the choke until the oxygen mix was right and the engine roared to life.

She had no idea how to steer a boat. "I'll get the ropes," she yelled. Lori quickly untied the thick nylon ropes wrapped around the metal spurs in the boat's berth and threw them back into the boat. Then she jumped in after them. "Do you need me to push away from the dock?"

"Yes. Do it fast."

The little boat rocked violently, and between the push and the bumps from getting up to speed, Lori needed to hang onto the side for fear of being thrown overboard. "What's the plan?" she shouted over the noise.

"Grab the kid before he falls off."

It was simple and direct. She could work with that.

Mac slowed as they approached the air mattress. Terrified brown eyes turned to them. They were a good ten feet away from the floatie, but they couldn't get closer without the risk of upsetting it. "Be still," Mac said.

It was good advice. Unfortunately, the recipient looked to be a six-year-old in a full panic. The little boy reached towards the boat. He slipped in slow motion, then slid into the water with a splash.

"Crap!"

"I've got him!" Lori toed off her shoes as she spoke. She dropped her phone on the seat and jumped in.

"Cold!" The word burst from her lips as every bit of heat was instantly sucked out of her body. The little boy in front of her was splashing frantically. She reached out and grabbed the back of his shirt. "Got you!"

It was only a few strokes back to the boat, but the kid didn't make it easy. Mac reached over the side to grab the boy's arm, but he didn't have the leverage to pull him aboard one-handed. Lori didn't have the angle to offer much help.

"Give me a sec." Her teeth chattered with the effort. "Five. Four. Three." Then she dropped, allowing herself to submerge so she could make buoyancy work in her favor. She grabbed the boy's waistband and heaved as she tried to lift her whole body out of the water with powerful kicks. She went under again quickly, but when she surfaced, the little boy was half over the side, his little legs kicking frantically until they disappeared as Mac finished hauling him into the boat.

"You're next," Mac said.

Lori nodded, then ducked once again. This time, with both hands on the side of the boat, she was able to get enough power to get her elbows hooked over the sides. "I'm not proud," she gasped. "Grab my belt and pull me in."

She pushed, Mac heaved, and she ended up on the bottom of the boat, gasping for air and beside a little boy who was yelling that they had to go back for his air mattress.

"No way, kid. We'll grab it when it blows back to shore. Your lips are turning blue," Mac said.

He bypassed the marina and headed for the beach. A pair of frantic parents slogged into thigh-high water to pull their son into their arms, babbling thanks. Lori barely had time to say they were welcome when Mac pulled away.

"Where are we going?"

"Back to the docks so I can drive you home. The kid isn't the only one turning blue from the cold."

The breeze coming off the lake added to her chills. Her hands shook too hard to help re-tie the boat. Men she didn't know did it for her; they were waiting on the dock when Mac returned. They helped the two of them off the boat, then stood aside as Mac ushered her to his truck that was parked on the street.

"I'm going to drip all over your seats."

He gave her a funny look. "They've seen worse. Get in."

Lori's teeth were chattering too much to talk, and Mac didn't have anything to say. He walked her all the way to her door. "Have a shower and relax. That water is freezing. I'll check on you later."

"Thanks."

While part of her brain was cognizant that this morning's paint would be dry since it had been more than two hours, another part of her turned on the fan and left the door open as she had the hottest, steamiest shower in human history. She didn't stay under the spray long, just enough to thoroughly chase away the chill. Then she ignored the sun streaming through the window, crawled under her comforter, and closed her eyes.

The next thing she knew, somebody was knocking on her door. Lori stumbled to her feet. "Coming!"

The sun was no longer shining through her window, and her brief glimpse of sky was orange and not blue. She'd slept the afternoon away. She didn't dare look in the bathroom mirror as she walked past the door, feeling how wild her hair was. At least she'd managed to put on fresh clothes before she'd fallen asleep.

The peephole showed a couple she didn't recognize— a beautiful, brown-eyed woman in a headscarf, and a man in his thirties with salt-and-pepper hair and a military posture. "Can I help you?" she asked through the door.

"It's okay. They're with me." Although she couldn't see Lucy, she recognized her voice. Lori opened the door and the couple beamed at her. "Hi. I'm Tripp Turner. This is my wife, Habibah Gamal. We own the Atlas Restaurant. The little guy you and Mac plucked out of Star Lake this afternoon is my nephew. There's no way we can thank you properly, but Mac said you got chilled when you went into the water. The least we could do was bring you some soup to warm you up." He held out a plastic bag.

"Thank you." She opened it and saw a large container of soup and a large package wrapped in aluminum foil.

"It's turkey vegetable. We also threw in some fresh rolls and butter," Habibah said.

Lori's stomach rumbled to life at the words. "It sounds delicious."

"Are you alright after your polar dip? Any bad effects?" the other woman asked.

"I think I'm good. Mac drove me straight home. I had a hot shower and fell right into bed. I'm wide awake now." It was true. She had all her energy back. She was hungry, but she'd slept for so long she doubted if she'd fall asleep before midnight.

"We're very glad to hear it," Tripp said. "If there's anything we can do, just ask. Aiden is my sister's only child. If it hadn't been for you and Mac..."

"I didn't even ask. Is Aiden alright?"

"He's perfectly fine. Complaining you didn't retrieve his air mattress. His father has said that since he wasn't supposed to go into the water without adult supervision, he's lost privileges for a month, so it doesn't matter."

"I'm glad to hear it. About him being fine, not the grounding."

They laughed with her. "We'll let you eat while it's hot," Habibah said. "We have to deliver some to Mac too."

"Thanks again."

They waved and left, but Lucy replaced them in the doorway. "Half the town knows what you did. Thank you."

"Of course!" Lori said.

"Are you sure you're okay?"

"Positive. Thanks."

The soup was as delicious as it smelled and returning to the Atlas moved up on her to-do list. Lori was still on a budget, but with all the walking she was doing instead of spending the money on gas, she could afford to treat herself to a nice meal after she received her first paycheck in a week.

It gave her something to look forward to.

And for a second, she wondered if she should invite Mac to eat with her.

CHAPTER 10

THE SMALL OFFICE had a table and four chairs for meeting clients, two desks and two chairs for him and Doug, a filing cabinet, a large storage room, and a bathroom in the back. The converted garage wasn't much, but they didn't spend much time in the headquarters of Mackenzie Brothers Painting.

It was big for two people. It was cavernous for one, which left Mac worried since his brother was half an hour late.

Lori, of course, was right on time. She was loading the van with the paint she and Doug needed for the day's job. The Pham girls were finally getting their bedrooms done. Seven-year-old Shelly wanted pink. June had finally settled on a geometric design they'd already purchased the paint for, and to her mother's delight, the rest of the walls were going to be vanilla white. It was going to be a two-day job, and Helen had promised the girls would be camping out in the basement, so Doug and Lori had free rein to move all the furniture as needed.

He was reaching for his phone to text his brother again when a series of messages popped onto the screen.

"Remember that chili you told me to throw out on Thursday?"

"I thought it would make it to Sunday."

"I was wrong."

"Won't be in today. Tomorrow's not looking good either."

"Sorry."

What could he say to that? He could call Doug an idiot for eating bad leftovers. but that wouldn't make his brother feel better or magically make another set of hands appear.

Lori appeared in the doorway. "I'm loaded. Will Doug be meeting me there?"

"Nope, he called in sick. It'll be you and me today."

"Oh."

He understood the sentiment behind the syllable. He wouldn't be very helpful. But it was all he could offer. "We'll make it work. Let's go."

She didn't complain. Instead, she nodded and asked if he wanted her to drive.

The Pham house was a nice bungalow. Helen and her husband had already shifted the twin beds and dressers into the center of the respective rooms, giving them lots of space to set up. Mac tossed Lori a roll of green tape. "You get started. I'll bring in everything else."

It was painful. Not the physical act of carrying the stuff, but not being able to do everything he used to. He couldn't even paint the trim since he didn't have the dexterity with his left hand for the precision needed.

Lori didn't waste time on chitchat. She simply went to work.

Mac slipped out to the van for a moment to text Doug. "Is she mad at me, or does she not talk?"

"She doesn't talk during setup. She's a machine. Let her do her thing."

He took his brother's advice. He was going to suggest an alternate order to the steps she was taking until he realized she was making things more difficult for herself to make them easier for him.

By the end of the first day, both rooms were taped, and they'd started painting the trim. The thing most people didn't understand when it came to painting was that the tiny detail work took most of the time. Once they could use rollers on clear swaths of wall, the rest of the room would be done in no time.

Mac was absolutely wiped, which surprised him considering how little he'd done. Lori had to be even more tired, but she didn't complain. "We'll finish tomorrow even if Doug isn't back, but it might be a late night," she predicted.

"That's fine," he said. "Unfortunately, we have to move right on to the Wachowski's main floor on Wednesday."

"I promise not to eat any week-old chili," she told him with a grin.

That was the first non-work-related comment she'd made all day. Lori Baker frustrated the life out of him. She was disaster-prone as a project manager who'd caused him nothing but grief when she'd worked next door. Then she helped him out after she was fired for no reason other than the fact she was there. She took a job she didn't have to with a painting company when she was a fully licensed architect. Then she went above and beyond when one of her bosses was out sick, but she didn't act like part of the team.

Exasperating. That's what she was. Especially since under all of that contradiction and beneath all of those prickles, she was a good person. She didn't think twice about jumping into a lake to save a kid she'd never met. She supported local charities when she wasn't local. She had great taste in music.

It was a real shame she worked for him.

Because now that she wasn't driving him nuts on a daily basis...

He kind of liked having her around.

CHAPTER 11

How cool was it that she had a place? When she walked into the Escape Room on Thursday after work, Emily motioned to her from behind the bar and pointed to an empty stool, pulling her a beer and ordering her not to move until they discussed the latest *Santa Monica, E.R.* episode. Lori had lived in downtown Minneapolis for three years and gone to the same corner bar on payday Fridays during that whole time, yet the waitresses never recognized her.

Then Rachel from the coffee shop waved to her from across the room. Even Julie Handler and her girlfriend acknowledged her with a nod. "Everybody knows," Emily told her.

"Knows?"

"That you went into the lake after Aiden. And that you covered for Doug when he was sick this week so June could have her bedroom done in time for her sleepover this weekend."

"Does this mean I may not be the town pariah

anymore?" She hadn't done any of the things Emily mentioned with the specific goal of trying to improve her reputation, but she'd happily take it if it was a side effect.

"You're on the right track."

"Well, I'm here for at least two more weeks while Mac's arm is in a sling. Maybe I'll be able to turn my past into a bad memory by the time I leave."

Emily grasped her arm, her grin taking up most of her face. "You're going to be here for the show's season finale. Watch party! I'll schedule the day off. You bring the dessert."

"Deal." When she was done in Holiday Beach, she was definitely keeping Emily on her BFF list. A person couldn't have too many die-hard hospital drama fans on their contact list. Even better, her new friend confided she was an aspiring actress who'd actually been on the set of *Santa Monica, E.R.* It was as a contest winner, not as an actress, but Emily promised to show her some pictures from backstage.

A gentle tap on Lori's shoulder interrupted her speculation about the fate of several doctors on the show. "Hi, Rachel."

"Hi, Lori. Sorry to interrupt, but I'm going to ask a favor."

"Ask away."

"My darts partner can't make it today, and I need a girl for our girls-against-guys match. Can you stand in? It won't be longer than an hour." The soft-spoken brunette looked over her shoulder at Owen.

"I'd love to help, but I don't play darts."

"That's okay. Mac has to throw left-handed because of his sling, so you'll be at the same skill level. Please say yes! We've been playing since the beginning of the year, and I don't want to break our streak."

"Sure." Why not? It would be a fun way to spend the evening. Better than sitting alone in her apartment again. "I hope Mac will be okay with me beating him. Or accidentally using him as a pincushion. You never know."

"We'll tell him to leave his boss badge outside."

Rachel ushered her to the corner where a series of dartboards hung on the wall. The barista pointed out the tape on the floor she had to stand behind, then explained the rules.

"You mean I have to aim for a certain number? I figured I'd aim for the dartboard in general and let Lady Luck take her chances," Lori joked.

"You can't do that," Mac said.

Her eyes went wide.

"That's my plan with my bum hand. No copying." He grinned at his own joke.

"I'm going to copy you and you can't stop me," she teased back.

She was terrible. Mac was worse.

"The board. Aim for the board!" Owen shouted at his partner. This was after Mac's second dart missed entirely and bounced off the wooden frame around the board's cork background.

"It's not my fault. The darts are malfunctioning," he grumbled good-naturedly.

"They do tend to do that. What with their moving parts and all," Lori agreed.

Then, when she was next up, the paper flight tucked into the slits at the end of her dart fell off and her dart bounced off the wall two feet from the ground.

"They're definitely malfunctioning," she said before

taking a big gulp of her drink to hide her embarrassed flush.

The very next round, she took careful aim and, with deliberate motions, threw another dart. It struck and stuck in the tiny wire arc of the triple-20 slot.

"Woo-hoo!" She didn't say she'd been aiming for the bullseye. She hugged Rachel in excitement. Then Owen pulled himself and Mac into the celebration. She tried to ignore the fact Mac gave good hugs. The truth was, she was lucky her next two darts hit the board for a total of eight more points, because she was still thinking about Mac's arms around her.

The game was an hour and twenty minutes because it took so long for either team to reach the winning score of a thousand and one points.

"I'm sorry we lost." Lori owed Rachel an apology. She'd missed the board more often than she'd hit it, leaving Rachel to do most of the scoring.

"Are you kidding? This is the closest match we've had since Lucy substituted for Mina on St. Patrick's Day. She kept distracting Roy by flashing her engagement ring at him and yelling that the diamond fell out," Rachel said.

"That would do it." The bar owner was obviously smitten with his fiancée.

"Win or lose, I appreciate you playing with me. I had fun."

"Me too. Thanks for asking." She meant it. Lori was going to be sorry to leave once her job at Mackenzie Brothers Painting was over. She wanted to get back into architecture, but she doubted she'd ever land in a place this friendly again.

She did regret one thing from the evening. She'd had much too much fun with Mac. Even if she didn't have to work with him again the next day, now she knew he had great taste in music and bad taste in beer. He was good at darts and was even better at making her laugh. But he was off-limits while she was in town and out of reach when she returned to the city.

Life was really unfair sometimes.

CHAPTER 12

"HURRAY FOR PAYDAY!" Doug exclaimed as Mac handed out the envelopes in the office on Friday after they'd finished for the day.

"My bank account agrees," Lori said.

Mac folded his and slipped it into his back pocket. "Everybody, meaning Lori, did great working extra hours to keep us on schedule this week. Thank you very much for really stepping up. Hopefully next week we'll be back to more regular hours. We're booked solid for the rest of the summer, so no more bad chili, Doug."

His brother put his hand on his stomach and groaned. "I promise."

"Now let's go enjoy our weekend. It's supposed to be fantastic weather. There's only one more after this before Memorial Day weekend when the tourists start arriving in droves. I, for one, intend to get a lot of fishing in," Mac said. "How about you two?"

"I'm going to finish painting the apartment so I can enjoy the various events of the long weekend," Lori said.

"I've got to head into Minneapolis tonight to do a

supply run. I'll be back late tomorrow afternoon, but I should be able to join you on the boat on Sunday morning," Doug told him.

"If you need to borrow any equipment, go ahead. Just let us know before you take it," Mac said to Lori.

"I could use some roller-tray liners," she said.

Doug winced. "Those are on the list to buy tomorrow."

"It's okay. I have some at my place. Do you want to swing by in the morning?" Mac asked. "I'll leave them on the front porch in case I'm already on the water by then."

"That would be great. Thanks."

Mac spent the evening organizing his tackle box and stretching his left shoulder to ensure he had full range for casting in the morning. Freedom day, when he could lose the sling, couldn't come fast enough. "Only two more weeks," he told himself as he carefully swung his left arm like a propeller.

Saturday morning dawned clear and bright, and he was at the marina as the sun cleared the treetops. Unwilling to fight with the motor on his own, Mac flicked open a collapsible lawn chair at the end of the dock, set his tackle box on one side and his coffee thermos on the other, and got to work.

Three hours later, he had an empty thermos, an empty fish stringer, and a full heart. As he walked back to his car, Roger Dresser gave him a wave. "How was your luck?" the marina owner asked.

"Not a bite."

"Good morning then?" The old man grinned at him knowingly.

"Very." It took another fisherman to know the purpose of fishing wasn't always to catch fish.

Mac wasn't surprised to see another vehicle in his driveway when he got home. He was surprised it wasn't Lori. He followed the voices around to the back of his property, his temper growing with every step as yet another set of strangers had invaded his home. He had no proof, but he was sure his new neighbors were to blame.

He found two men at the far end of his backyard, standing under the boughs of the poplars that bordered his property. The older one, a white man with whiter hair and a fishing vest Mac couldn't help but envy, was pointing at his roof. The younger one, a darker skinned man in a T-shirt and rugged cargo pants, was focusing a long camera lens at Mac's chimney.

"Can I help you?" he called.

"Just admiring the view," the older man replied.

"I can see that. What I meant was, who are you and why are you taking pictures of my house?" Mac said.

"Kurt Crabb. Kurt with a K and Crabb with two Bs and no E. *Modern Minnesota* magazine. This is my photographer, Brent Byles," he said. He pulled a business card out of a vest pocket, and Mac confirmed his information matched the names on the card. What Kurt Crabb hadn't said was he was credited as the senior editor. "We're doing a piece on eco-friendly construction, and I have to say this new build does not disappoint, Mister...?"

"Mackenzie. Bob Mackenzie. How did you happen to find out about my place?"

"Lorelei Baker."

Mac had to laugh. He *knew* she was somehow involved. "Of course."

"I know you weren't expecting us right now. I convinced Brent to drive up early to try to get some fishing in this afternoon. Is there any chance of a tour? We'd love to see what you've done on the inside."

There wasn't anything inside he was worried about. Most of his furnishings were still in storage. Besides, he wasn't about to miss a chance to show off his baby to people who obviously had great taste in houses.

As they walked back to the front door, they discussed the cooling benefits of his ash-gray metal roof and the eavestrough and drainage system designed to capture rain runoff. The black-framed triple-paned windows were specifically placed to take advantage of morning and evening light without overheating the house during the hottest days of summer.

Kurt paused at the front door. "Was this in the original design?"

"No. I decided on a smaller deck than I'd first planned on because the sliding doors in the back exit right onto the patio. This way I can still have a coffee and enjoy the lake view without having a massive platform for entertaining on the front of the house," Mac explained as he led them inside.

Brent made a beeline to the cast-iron woodstove in the corner. "What a beauty! What will you be using for a heat shield?"

Mac agreed with the assessment. "Cement board with slate tiles, but it's going to have a large base, so the stovepipe does most of the work," Mac said. He hadn't installed anything yet because he'd been delayed in getting the cement board. Now he was waiting to have the proper wall material installed, and then the walls and floor tiled before he lifted the four-hundred-pound stove into place. Once it was in and installed, it could heat most of the house in the winter, especially since his bedroom was directly above that corner.

"You've made a lot of eco-friendly choices," Kurt noted.

The bamboo floors, the LED pot lights, the high-efficiency appliances. Mac had chosen everything with care. If he was creating something out of nothing, why wouldn't he pick things that would help protect the nature he loved so much?

"I'm not claiming to be an environmental saint. There's a steam shower in the upstairs suite strictly because it feels terrific after a long day at work. It sucks a lot of energy. The carport with the gravel pad behind the garage is for my boat and snowmobile. But I tried to compensate in other places," Mac said.

"Perfection is the enemy of done," Kurt said. "We at *Modern Minnesota* would rather see a useable home that's eighty percent efficient than plans for a house that's one hundred percent green and never gets built."

A knock on the open living-room door drew all their attention. "Mac?" Lori leaned through the doorway. Most of her black curls had escaped her ponytail. "Oh, sorry to interrupt. You said you were going to put the paint-tray liners on the porch."

"I forgot. Come in. I met some friends of yours outside."

She stepped over the threshold cautiously. "Friends of mine?"

"Kurt Crabb and Brent Byles of *Modern Minnesota*. They said you told them about my build."

Her blue eyes brightened in recognition of the names, but then clouded over again. "I know of them and of

Modern Minnesota magazine, but I never mentioned you, Mac."

Both men looked confused. "You're Lorelei Baker, one of the magazine's Green Home contest winners."

"Yes, I am. We met at the award presentation."

"And this is the Parkman project," Kurt continued.

"No, that is Bob Mackenzie, and this is his house. The Parkman property is next door." She looked directly at Mac and raised her hands in surrender.

All of a sudden, he understood how stuff kept happening to her. People made assumptions because of a lack of communication.

"No harm, no foul, as far as I'm concerned," Mac said. "I'm happy to show off my house. I'm just sorry I wasted your time."

"I'm not. We'd love to come back and see it when it's finished if you're interested," Kurt said graciously.

"Definitely."

Brent took another look around the main floor. "This is going to be spectacular."

"I hope so. It took long enough to build."

As they moved toward the door, Kurt said to Lori, "Why don't you come with us next door and show us around?"

"Unfortunately, I'm not working on the project anymore. I'm happy to discuss the original plans and design the Parkman project is based off, and they signed a release allowing me to do that. But I can't comment on the current build, any new designs, or the property. I'll point you in the right direction, though."

She walked them to their car and pointed at the roof, which was visible over the top of the copse on the property boundary. They talked for a few minutes and Kurt handed something to Lori. When she returned to the deck, her first words were, "I swear this isn't my fault."

"I know. It was a misunderstanding."

"Was Kurt at least polite about your house? Please tell me he didn't say anything rude."

Mac fist pumped with his good arm. "He really liked it. I think he meant it when he said he wants to come back to see it once it's done." Kurt's comments had been very validating. Mac had mostly designed the place himself. Years of seeing what worked and didn't in other people's houses had given him a lot of ideas and options. Aside from needing a professional to draw up the plans to be submitted and make some technical changes he hadn't known were required, his house was one hundred percent his.

"That's good. Except for the fact the Parkman project has intruded on your life. Again."

"Sadly, I'm getting used to it." He didn't want to her to feel bad, but he couldn't think of a way to change the conversation. "Paint-tray liners."

"Right!"

"How close are you to finishing your apartment?" he asked. Lucy had made a great deal with getting Lori to do the dirty work for her. Caleb, their part-time employee, had received a similar deal for the same studio apartment in the other building when Lucy and her friend Brooke had discovered the young man had been living in his car. Mac and Doug had helped him paint it the previous fall. Now the kid was doing well, working full-time at By the Cup and occasional shifts with them while he saved for a one-bedroom apartment. The little suite was probably better for Lori than a hotel room, although it had to be a step down from what she was used to. But he couldn't fault her for making a responsible choice when they couldn't guarantee her enough work to sign a regular contract.

"Pretty close. The walls are ready. Since it's just one room, I'll do one coat today, and maybe the second tonight if I can. Then it'll be ready for the next tenant, or Lucy can make her other updates."

His ears locked onto two words. "Next tenant? Are you not renewing your lease for another month?"

"Not yet. Lucy is holding it for me, but she's going to wait until the last minute. You could be back at work by then, so I don't want to commit to staying in Holiday Beach if I don't have anything lined up."

"Do you have anything back in the city?" She was fitting in so well with the company and in the community. He didn't want her to feel like he was driving her out.

"A bunch of "we'll keep your information on file; thank you for applying" emails," Lori said with a laugh. "But I'm hopeful. I'm also still sending out applications." She gave him a strained smile; he recognized the difference after seeing a real one after their darts game.

She deserved to catch a break. The best he could do was not delay her from getting her chores done at her apartment, so she could enjoy the rest of her weekend before they started yet another hectic week at work. "Good luck with the painting. See you Monday."

"Or sooner, if I catch you at the marina tomorrow."

"I'll bring my swimsuit."

"Go ahead. I'll stay on the dock!" she said as she walked out the door, leaving them both laughing.

CHAPTER 13

THIS WAS the third week of her four-week contract, and Lori was conflicted.

She liked her work. Rather, she liked the people she was working with—Mac and Doug were a lot of fun and were very fair bosses. She'd worked on three houses so far, and they'd all been interesting to study on an architectural level. The actual painting was hard, messy work that was not in her top ten favorite things to do at all.

She missed her desk and her computer and dreaming of blueprints drawn in one-quarter inch to one-foot ratios. The conversation she'd had with Kurt Crabb about Mac's house was the first time she'd had a chance to use her education in weeks. The pain of having to ignore it to earn a paycheck hit her like a brick.

As much as she liked Holiday Beach, and her new friends like Emily, Gloria, Lucy...and Mac, she didn't think she could stay. The town didn't need a full-time architect, even if she had the money to open her own firm.

Which made her short chat with Kurt even more interesting. He asked her if she was interested in doing a piece for *Modern Minnesota* about the vacation rental industry in the area. She'd have to research cottages and summer homes around Star Lake. The pay was minimal, and the piece was only for their online edition, but a small paycheck was better than nothing, especially when it didn't interfere with her day job. She'd told him she'd think about it, but she'd already made up her mind.

"Say hello to Lori Baker, reporter and photographer for *Modern Minnesota*," she said to her reflection in the mirror.

Now all she needed was a list of cottages to photograph and a story idea.

None had magically appeared by Monday morning when she arrived at the Mackenzie Brothers office. Instead, she walked in to Mac miming throttling somebody while he calmly spoke on the phone.

"But I need them now, not in two months. That's why I ordered them four months ago," Mac said. From his tone, she could tell it wasn't the first time he'd said that. "Sales rep," he mouthed to her in explanation. "No, I tried your online chat bot. It told me to email your customer-service line. They sent me an email telling me I'd get a call within two business days. That was last Tuesday. So now I'm calling you, the person who sold them to me and the person I gave my money to, because I know your company name to leave an online review. Where are my glass railings?" he asked. Then a pause. "If you know they were sent to the wrong location, can't you pick them up and send them on to me?"

It sounded like a reasonable request to Lori. Especially if they were only misdirected.

"What do you mean, they were installed at the wrong address?"

She flinched at his voice suddenly doubling in volume. "Then cancel the order and give me my money back! You just told me they wouldn't even be fabricated for another month."

Lori knew what he was talking about. Mac had rhapsodized about the glass railings he'd ordered for the split staircase that ran in two halves in front of the wall that divided his living room from the downstairs bedroom. The glass was supposed to enhance the open feel of the main floor. But it sounded like they were a far-off dream at this point. Or a nightmare. At least she had nothing to do with this disaster.

"No, cancel the order. I'll expect the email within the hour for the cancellation and full refund on my credit card. Thank you for your help." He set the receiver on the office phone with a little more oomph than necessary. "Well, glass railings are now out of the question. I don't want wooden or iron pickets. It's either go without for months or come up with a fast solution." He turned his honey-brown eyes on her. "Any ideas?"

"Not off the top of my head, but I'll think on it for you."

"I'd appreciate it. I have an appointment in Bixby this morning, but I'll swing by the Wyatts at lunch to see how things are going," Mac said.

She let the idea simmer in the back of her mind as she and Doug taped and prepared the living room, dining room, and hallway of a bungalow on the edge of town. Gene and Jean Wyatt had excitedly met them at the door. "Come in and please fix this lilac nightmare," the white-haired Jean pleaded.

"You wanted the lilac. You specifically requested the

lilac. Why are you complaining about the lilac?" her husband grumbled good-naturedly.

"That was the nineties! I've wanted to get rid of it for twenty years."

"You could have said something a decade ago."

Jean looked at them. "Please ignore the blood spatter as I kill him. For years he said we'd do it ourselves, but he was always too busy. I finally talked him into it and then he fell off the ladder this fall cleaning the gutters. He may not live to see the final result if he keeps teasing me."

Lori loved the bickering. It reminded her of her maternal grandparents. "What color are we changing the lilac to?" Doug asked.

"Sandstone with an accent wall of forest green," Gene said.

"Sounds lovely. Let's get to it," Lori said.

Jean pointed out the full coffeepot on the kitchen counter, and the two seniors promptly escaped to a screened-in back deck with their coffees.

She and Doug worked in a companionable silence as they moved furniture and prepared the room. By the time Mac showed up, they'd just started taping the window trim.

"All good?" Doug asked.

"I sat in the waiting room for an hour and a half and was then told I'd have to reschedule because of an emergency. I'm going back tomorrow."

"You are having a terrible day."

"Tell me about it," Mac grumped.

"I have a suggestion for your house that might cheer you up," Lori offered. The quiet morning had given her time to puzzle over Mac's quandary. There were dozens of things he could do to a staircase, and she had studied them all. But she eliminated most of them immediately. Mac's house was practically perfect, and she didn't want to detract from that with a lesser idea.

The open concept was the challenge. He needed something that would maintain it while still meeting the safety code. One idea kept popping up.

"What is it?"

"Have you considered doing a wooden slat wall? Stained, not painted. All the way to the ceiling. I'm thinking of one by six-inch boards."

He just stared at her.

Shoot. She'd thought it was a great compromise between safety and sight lines. The gaps between the evenly spaced boards would allow people looking straight on to see all the way through the wall. But from the side, they'd provide a textured effect. Plus, it would get some wood on the wall to continue the warmth of natural materials in the house. "Or not."

"That could be a brilliant idea."

"I have pictures!" She whipped out her phone and showed him the saved images. They discuss the benefits of broad spacing versus the cleaner but narrow look of using standard two-by-twos.

"I think this deserves a lunch. My treat, obviously, for saving me from the catastrophe of having to figure out what kind of railing will be the least ugly."

When he returned her smile, something shifted in her gut. They'd been bumbling along on the same road for a while now, awkward and out of pace, ever since she'd first helped him down from the bar's roof and he'd offered her the job in return. Then they started moving side by side after she'd saved Aiden from the water. But now, for the first time, they'd clicked.

"I'd like that."

So, of course, his phone exploded in a series of chimes to signal incoming texts. Mac looked down in interest and then opened his brown eyes wide. "Can I offer you a rain check? They're able to see me in forty minutes. I can make it if I leave right now."

"Go!" She didn't even know what the appointment was for, but it was obviously important to him. "I'll be here when you get back. Hopefully with all the cutting-in done."

"It's a date. A date for a thank-you lunch for the idea," Mac stuttered before he bolted out the door.

"I'm betting he wishes he'd never hired you," Doug said from the dining room.

It was like she'd been thrown into Star Lake in January. His words sucked all the air out of her lungs. She thought they were at least friendly with each other. "What?"

"Mac likes you a lot. But he'll never date an employee. He hamstringed his own social life."

"Two weeks ago, he couldn't stand me."

"Two weeks ago, you were working for the Parkmans and driving everybody in town nuts with special requests for them. People change."

"Mac likes me? Are you sure?"

"Yep, but he'll never tell you as long as you're working for us. Which is good. Because he's your boss and that would be wrong. But it's nice you two are getting along now."

What a disaster! She'd finally found a nice guy and she couldn't date him. For all the right reasons. At least she only had to avoid her feelings and act like everything was fine for two more weeks. She could do that. She'd pretended with Mrs. Parkman for months.

"Come on, let's get back to it. Maybe we can start the first coat before we leave today," she said. If she worked hard enough, she might be distracted from the ideas about Mac running through her head.

But she doubted it.

CHAPTER 14

THE DOCTOR in the white coat on the far side of the room crossed her arms and stared at him in disbelief. "Tell me again."

"I haven't done anything!" Mac was desperate for her to believe him. He'd already sat in the waiting room, had an X-ray, and suffered through countless tests. He'd been there for hours. "I yanked the pull start on my boat half a dozen times before somebody stopped me, but I did it left-handed. I did paint trim and some cutting-in for two days last week, but also with my left hand. My right arm never left the sling. I swear! Why? What happened?"

"What happened is that your shoulder is healing at a phenomenal rate. Which means you have been listening to me and resting it, which, knowing you, is highly unlikely," Dr. Barbara White said.

Mac wanted to argue, but it was a fair observation. Dr. White had been a general physician in Bixby for thirty years since she first started working at the only hospital in the area. She'd known Mac since the first time he'd broken his arm dirt biking. By the third time, she stopped with the concerned aunt routine and laid into him like the reckless kid he'd been.

This felt like he'd surprised his teacher by getting an "A" and she wasn't sure if he'd been cheating. "How have you avoided using it at work?" she asked.

"By avoiding work. Doug and Lori have banished me to the office. I only got to be on-site for those two days when Doug came down with food poisoning." Doug didn't know it, but Mac owed him for that unintended favor. First, it got him out of the office for a couple days, and he'd desperately needed the break for his mental health. It also gave him some time with Lori. But she was a problem for another time.

The doctor didn't look up from the notes she was writing in his file. "Well, keep it up. I told you four weeks was the minimum you'd be out, but I honestly expected it to be eight. If you keep resting it like you have been, I'll be confident to let you go back to work by the end of the month," Dr. White said.

"I will."

"I mean it, Mac. Don't blow it now and try to work ahead. That whole "exercise will make it stronger" line is baloney. Resting your injury will let it fully heal. Then you can make it stronger."

"I'll rest it. I promise." Not doing anything was a lot harder than it sounded. He swore half his headaches were from the stress on his brain constantly telling his body not to twist, pull, or push with his bad arm. At least the pain was minimal now. He could do it for another two weeks. It beat the option of having to do it for four weeks with extra pain after he reinjured himself.

"Good. Come back at the end of next week and I'll give you the all-clear to go back to work. It's looking good."

By the time he was back in his truck, Mac knew it was going to be the end of the workday before he got back to the office. He sent a quick text to Doug and Lori, telling them he'd see them in the morning. Then he headed back to Holiday Beach to celebrate his good news in a way that was healthy.

"A double scoop, please. Chocolate and Oreo," Mac ordered at the counter of Lakeside Cones and Sundaes. The ice cream shop was the mirror image of By the Cup. A long counter with two freezers full of a variety of flavors sat in front of another counter full of cones and toppings. A few small round tables lined the other wall, each with a pair of chairs. He was the only customer in the place, which made sense since it was five o'clock. Too late for after school snacking and too early for dessert.

"That's going to spoil your dinner."

Correction. He was one of two customers in the joint. Lori had been behind a large inflatable palm tree, he just hadn't seen her. "No, this is my supper."

"Mac, you're a grown-up."

"Ice cream is made from milk and cream, which has calcium in it and is good for bones. My bones need all the help they can get. This is health food," he argued. It was a ridiculous argument, but it had the desired effect.

Lori burst into laughter. "I can't argue with science."

"You really can't. But what's your excuse?" he asked.

"Here you go, Lori," the sundae barista said, setting a pint carton on the glass freezer case.

She smiled like she'd been called on by a teacher and

knew the answer. "I'm being good. This is going to be dessert."

"What did you get?"

"Burgundy cherry."

He pulled a face. He wasn't even trying to flirt. That flavor was simply too gruesome to eat. "That's granny ice cream."

"How dare you, sir!" She nodded at the barista and grabbed her treasure. "It has cherries in it; therefore, it is a serving of fruit. Not," she sneered at him, "chocolate and cookies."

"Okay. Technically, it's fruit and dairy," Mac conceded.

A horn outside beeped. "That's for me," Lori said.

"Do you have a date?"

"A double date. Me and Chris Carmichael and Emily and Cameron Irvine." She grinned at him. "It's the *Santa Monica, E.R.* season finale tonight, so Emily and I are having a watch party. I'm supplying the dessert."

The girl behind the counter called his name. "I'll let you get to your supper before it melts," Lori said. She stopped at the door. "Hey, how did your appointment go?"

"All good," he said.

"Great. See you tomorrow."

Great. It was true. Doctor White had given him terrific news that meant he'd be back to work in a couple of weeks. Which meant Lori would soon be out of work. But what could he do about it? They'd both been clear from the outset. This wasn't a long-term gig. They'd given each other the time they'd promised. They didn't owe each other anything.

Mac took his gigantic waffle cone down the beach.

Lori had to get back to her real life in Minneapolis, anyway. If she was staying in Holiday Beach and had a job where she wasn't working for him, he might spend more time thinking about things. But she wasn't, so he needed to concentrate on other things. Like ice cream.

CHAPTER 15

"I DON'T UNDERSTAND why burgundy cherry gets such a bad rap," Lori said as she doused her bowl of ice cream in chocolate syrup.

Emily recoiled in horror. "Maybe because you do things like that to it!"

Poor choice in ice cream toppings aside, Emily Jardine had been a bright light during Lori's stay in Holiday Beach. She was going to miss her new friend when her time here was done. Although they'd started their friendship bonding over television shows, they'd quickly discovered they had much more in common.

"Don't judge. Now tell me everything," Lori said as she settled into the corner of Emily's sofa. They had fifteen minutes of entertainment news to get through before the season finale of *Santa Monica, E.R.* started.

She was talking about Emily's trip to the set of their favorite show, where she got to watch them film an episode and met some of the cast in person.

"I talked to Cameron Irvine and Marki Queen and took pictures with them. Peter Spock was on set that day, but I didn't have a chance to meet him." Emily fanned her dark face with a well-manicured hand at the memory.

"That sounds incredible. What did you think of seeing what happens behind the scenes?" Lori wasn't sure if she wanted to know the magic that went into her favorite shows. She was afraid it might take away from their entertainment value.

Emily beamed. "It was very cool. I was so happy. And so unbelievably jealous."

"Jealous?"

"All I've ever wanted to be is an actress. But I had a late start, and I only have a little training. I can barely afford the occasional course at the local community college. I keep auditioning, but I haven't had any luck. Not for theater, not for commercials. Nothing." Emily sighed deeply. "Hardly anybody in town takes me seriously. Except Roy. But I am serious. After my trip to L.A., I came back and signed up for another acting class. Then I contacted the director at the dinner theater south of St. Cloud and asked for the chance to audition for their next show. And I contacted every single casting agent in Minneapolis and St. Paul. I even sent some headshots to a place in Chicago. I've never been more terrified in my life." Emily's big chocolate-brown eyes were wide in fear, even though she was just retelling her story.

"What happened?"

"I got representation. I told them I'd be game for anything as long as I got to keep my clothes on."

"Congratulations! That's huge." Emily putting herself out there for auditions was much harder than Lori applying for jobs. Emily was going to get way more rejections. But she sounded excited about the prospect. "What about your bartending job?"

"Roy likes to tease, but he's really a good boss. He's given me time off before when I needed it. I came home from California last year and told him I was going to try acting again and he promised to give me whatever time off I need for auditions."

"That's pretty cool." Lori did some math in her head. "It's been almost a year since your trip, right? How has it been going?"

"Three commercial auditions, and one line in a locally filmed Christmas movie last fall."

"That's fantastic!"

"In a year, it's not great."

Lori didn't know how to respond to that. She didn't know the industry. She didn't even know Emily that well. But she wanted to be supportive. "I think it's great you are going after your dream. Even if your success is only coming in small drops, it's still coming. I hope you don't quit."

"Thanks." Emily clinked Lori's ice cream bowl with her own. "Here's to more auditions in the future. Maybe someday I'll be back on the *Santa Monica, E.R.* set in front of the camera."

"I'll eat to that."

"And you'll be on the cover of an architectural magazine. Well, one of your houses will be," Emily said.

Lori licked a cherry off the back of her spoon. "Not any time soon, I won't be. I thought I had a shot with the Parkman house, and the whole town knows how that one turned out." It had been almost a month and she hadn't had a single response from any of her emails or applications. She'd even branched into neighboring states looking for work.

"I'll bet your original design was brilliant."

"It was. The plans for the other finalists were good too, but I had a good shot of winning the contest. But it's not a total loss. It got my name in front of the magazine's editor, and he remembered it. If I'm really lucky, this assignment will lead to more. At least it's related to my degree." A list of published articles in prominent magazines would fill the holes on her résumé while she was between jobs.

"Hold up. What assignment?" Emily demanded.

"Some people from *Modern Minnesota*, including the editor, were in Holiday Beach to look at the Parkman project. They went to Mac's place by mistake."

Emily snorted. "Sorry, but that sounds like his luck. What happened?"

"The editor recognized my name. When I told him I wasn't working for the Parkmans anymore, he offered me an assignment. Photos and an article about the cottage industry around Star Lake."

"Did you take it?"

"Of course! I'm not turning down paying work. I've already picked out the cottages I want to shoot. They're listed as part-time rentals. I'm just waiting for some owners to get back to me to give permission to feature them." It hadn't been easy working around her day job with Mac, but Lori had woken early to get some sunrise shots of two places, and sunset shots of three more. With the two places she'd scoped out on Sunday, she had five profiles to send to Kurt Crabb as well as two spares in case the cottage owners didn't want to be featured in the magazine. It was an easy paycheck. It was too bad it couldn't be a consistent one. She was putting together pitches for future article ideas, though. It was a great side job to supplement her regular full-time job. When she finally got one.

"Aren't you going to stay on with Mackenzie Brothers Painting?"

"No. This was always a temporary thing until Mac got better or I got another job. It's looking like Mac will beat me to the punch."

"That stinks."

Lori shrugged. "They did me a favor. Even with paying for a month's rent, I earned enough to cover my bills and add to my cushion while I return to the job hunt. I should send out another bunch of emails tomorrow night."

"Well, good luck," Emily said. "To both of us. We're good, hardworking women. We deserve some luck. I want to make my mark on the whole world."

"Today, Holiday Beach. Tomorrow, all of Minnesota. The day after, the world."

"That's the plan. Now, no talking until the commercial break. My boyfriend is about to grace my television with his presence." Emily stuffed a spoonful of burgundy cherry into her mouth and leaned forward on her cushion.

Lori did the same.

Careers were great, but a girl had her priorities on season finale night. Hot actors and cold desserts were at the top of the list.

CHAPTER 16

"What are we going to do?" Mac had sat on his news for three days before it exploded out of his mouth. He was going back to work. In the game of employment musical chairs, Lori, the woman who'd saved his bacon twice, was going to end up without a seat.

"We? I think you mean what are *you* going to do? You're the older brother and the senior partner. You should be the one to tell her," Doug insisted.

"Come on. Be a pal."

"I'm not going to fire Lori." His brother held up his hands and backed away.

"We aren't firing her. We're telling her that her short-term contract isn't being extended after next week, just like we originally discussed." It sounded perfectly logical and polite. It felt like anything but.

"This sucks," Doug said.

"It does. But we can't afford to keep her on. If we tell her now, we're giving her time to start looking again. It's the best bad choice we have," Mac insisted. This is why he liked being a small business owner with only two employees. He'd never fire his brother. More workers meant decisions like this. It was a terrible situation.

"You're right. We should just tell her. And give her an amazing reference letter."

"Then it's agreed. I'll tell her," Mac said. He'd tell her how awesome she'd been, and how much he appreciated her. He could also say that he liked her and wanted to take her out when he was no longer her boss, although that last part may not work since she wouldn't be in Holiday Beach anymore.

"Tell me what?"

It was the sneakers with the paint splashes. They turned Lori into a ninja, allowing her to sneak up on him. He opened his mouth, but nothing came out. He wasn't prepared for this.

"Mac?"

This was worse than ripping a bandage off one of his hairy shins, but fast was the way to do it so as not to draw out the pain. "The doctor said I'll be back at work in a week and a half. Next Friday will be your last day, Lori. I'm really sorry." He took a breath to make it through the rest of it. How great she'd been, how much he'd—they'd—miss her, they'd be sure to give her a great reference, let—

"I figured you'd be back to work sooner rather than later with all that health food you've been eating," she said, a small smile gracing her face. It wasn't much, but it reached her shining blue eyes. "It's okay, Mac. I suspected it was coming. That's what we agreed to. I really can't ask for anything more, especially since working for Mackenzie Brothers gave me a chance to make some repairs to my reputation in Holiday Beach."

"Are you sure? We'll write you an excellent letter of recommendation," he offered eagerly. How fast the tables had turned. Less than a month ago, he would have been the first to discourage anyone from hiring Lori Baker. Now he was a huge fan. "Do you have any jobs lined up?"

"Actually..." Her voice trailed off, and a flush rose up her cheeks.

"Please tell us so we don't feel so bad," Doug begged.

"Unless the Parkmans are hiring you back. Then lie," Mac said.

"Remember Kurt Crabb?" she asked him. He nodded. "He offered me an assignment for his magazine. I've been working on it in the evening. I'm going to see if he has anything else planned while I continue to look for interviews."

"Well, that's something," he said hopefully. It was better than being completely unemployed.

"It's a start. And it's architecture."

"So you have a new job to go to. Sort of."

"I do. So don't feel guilty. We helped each other out."

"We did."

"And we still have seven more days of painting. Where are we off to today?"

Doug picked a sheet off Mac's desk. "It's a multiday job. We're doing the exterior of Thunder Lanes." At her puzzled look, his brother added, "It's the local bowling alley. Mac's coming along to sign for the scaffolding that's already been set up."

"It's supposed to be another glorious week of sunshine. How do you guys always manage that?" she asked.

"Good planning," Doug said. "Which is more than I can say for our paint order. I'm off to collect the second half from Julie, so you'll have to ride with Mac."

Mac blinked. He had intended to pick up the paint.

His baby brother was giving him time with Lori. As they climbed into his truck, he tried to organize his thoughts.

"I'm glad to hear you're going to have a full recovery, Mac. We weren't friends when I saw you fall off the roof and you still scared the life out of me. Your accident could have been so much worse than you just losing a month of work," Lori said.

"I was so lucky, and most of that was thanks to your quick response. I'm more worried about you now. Are you sure you're going to be alright?" he asked. He expected an answer about work, but he was also talking about her being okay personally. He didn't want Lori to feel like she'd been fired twice in two months.

"I will be fine, Mac. Thank you for your concern, truly, but you can't be worried about me. You have your own business to watch. Besides, I'm getting more excited about this *Modern Minnesota* article. I was talking to Emily, and I think there may be more opportunities for me there."

"That's good. That Kurt guy seemed pretty friendly." Now he had more incentive than ever to invite the man back when the house was finished. He needed to put in a good word for Lori.

"It's an option I hadn't considered before. I'm looking into similar assignments with other magazines and websites."

He breathed easier, knowing she had options. He didn't have a chance to ask her any more questions because they were at their destination.

Thunder Lanes wasn't far from his office. The scaffolding had gone up on the outside the previous week when the stucco was being patched. The stucco company had partnered with Mac on the bid, leaving Mackenzie

Brothers Painting free to finish the job with a fresh coat of paint.

"What color is it going to be? More of the same?" Lori asked as she studied the two-story building that housed a bowling alley on the main floor and a series of apartments on the second.

It was currently mint green with cream trim. "Thankfully, yes," he said.

"Thankfully?"

"There was talk about switching it to a peachy color. We did a sample patch on the back of the building. It looked terrible." He shivered at the memory. "The owners felt the same way, so Thunder Lanes is going to stay green until the end of the decade."

"I've seen peach stucco before. It's never pretty."

"Right? Let's get you ready for when Doug gets back with the paint." Mac was backing into the spot by the service entrance when he noticed they had an audience. He parked and closed his door and was immediately assaulted by a hand poking him in the thigh.

"Did you really get hit by lightning?" his little attacker asked. The towheaded little boy looked at him with big eyes.

"Almost. It hit the roof I was working on, Richie." The little eyes went bigger.

"Are you 'lectric now? Daddy, we have to get a lightbulb!"

"Oh, kiddo," Owen groaned. "I told you, Mr. Mackenzie can't put a lightbulb in his mouth and make it glow like Chipper Munk in your cartoons."

"I really can't, Richie. Sorry. Only chipmunks can do that," Mac said, using his serious voice.

"Let's get a chipmunk!"

"Holly doesn't like mice. I don't think a cat would be a good friend to a chipmunk either. If we can only have one pet in the store, I think it should be Holly, don't you?" Mac liked the newcomer to Holiday Beach. Owen ran Golden Daye Antiques, Holiday Beach's number one used goods store, which he'd taken it over from his ailing grandfather. Mac wasn't an antiques person, but the fact Owen was dating Rachel meant they saw a lot of each other at the coffee shop.

Mac turned to Lori. "Holly's their cat."

"Thanks, Mac. I hadn't figured that out." Her smile betrayed her deadpan voice.

"We actually didn't stop to discuss your shocking event—" Owen started.

"Too late, Rachel already made that joke," Mac said.

"Shoot. Anyway, I wanted to ask if you were already on a team this weekend for the Picks and Pics walk. Do you want to hang out with Team Daye on Saturday afternoon for a couple of hours?" Owen asked. "You're welcome too, Lori."

"I figured out Holly was a cat, but I'm going to need somebody to explain Picks and Pics," she said.

"The Holiday Beach Parks Committee also takes care of the hiking and snowmobile trails around Holiday Beach. In the spring, we walk them with garbage bags to clean them up before the first tourists arrive to start the season off right. The town hires summer students who take over in July and August, but we all chip in to give them a head start. We collect the litter and take pictures of the trails to post on social media. Every group gets assigned a section of trail. It'll only take a couple of hours if you'd like to join us for a day of fresh air and nature," Owen said.

Mac had participated in the spring trail cleanup every year since it began. The "pics" part had only started in the last couple of years, when the Chamber of Commerce had begun offering prizes for the five photos that got the most votes on the town's website. "Sure, I'll come with you guys. I'm only half as effective as normal, so Richie will have to help me out. Okay, Richie?"

"I'm going to help," the little boy agreed.

"I'll help too," Lori said.

"Great. Rachel and I will bring the trash bags. You guys bring your cameras. We're leaving from the Bonfire Bay Campground at one o'clock on Saturday. Don't be late."

"Bye! Keep practicing with the lightbulb, Mr. Mac. You can do it if you try harder."

Lori snorted and didn't try to hide her laughter. Mac managed to give them a thumbs-up as the other pair walked away. "Don't you dare tell Doug."

"Of course I'm telling Doug!" she teased. "But seriously, are you okay with me hanging out with you on the weekend? The whole employer-employee socializing scenario?"

He nodded in understanding. "It's not like it's going to be a date. We'll be well chaperoned. I'm okay with it if you are." Backing away was the right thing to do, but it was difficult. If Lori stayed in Holiday Beach after she her stint at Mackenzie Brothers Painting, then he'd ask her out. But it didn't sound like she'd be around.

He didn't have time to ask her what her plans were, not that she'd had a chance to make any with the news that had landed in her lap this morning. All he could do was help her get organized on the jobsite and then give her time to find her feet before another piece of news rocked her.

But he had an idea that might offer her another opportunity. As soon as Doug arrived, he'd see if he could put it into action.

CHAPTER 17

FOR THE FIRST time since she'd been in Holiday Beach, the weekend dawned gray and wet. The forecast didn't offer much hope for Sunday either. "It's better now than on the long weekend," Lori muttered to herself.

She had a lazy morning, enjoying her freshly painted apartment until it was time to meet Mac and the others at the campground. She pulled on jeans and sneakers with rubber soles that stretched around to cover her toes. A windbreaker with a hood was all the protection she had from the drizzle unless she wanted to stroll through the woods with an umbrella. She could handle being damp for a couple of hours.

The others were waiting at the campground. The parking lot facing the playground and picnic area was filled with cars. Rachel waved to her from one of the picnic tables. "Don't panic. This is a staging area. We're taking the north shore trail from here to the gas station on the highway. It's about three miles. Owen's grandfather is going to pick us up when we call and drive us back to our cars."

The brunette coffee shop owner pointed out other groups and told her where they were going. Lori spotted Roy and Lucy heading south. "They're taking the trail that will pass behind the Dew Drop Inn. They'll have a longer walk than groups that have smaller legs like ours," Rachel said.

"I have small legs," Richie shouted.

"You do. We're going to use your small legs and our big legs to clean the trails so people can enjoy them over the summer," Rachel said.

"Did people litter? That's bad. And gross."

Owen zipped his son's jacket to block the wind off the lake. "Some people litter. Sometimes it's old trash that blows in on the wind and gets stuck in the bushes. Are you ready to go?"

"I'm ready," the little boy shouted.

"Me too."

Richie raced ahead. His father trailed behind, holding a garbage bag. Rachel grabbed the handle of a wagon on the far side of the picnic table and began to pull it behind her. "We're leaving bags of trash on the trails as we fill them. We have a team of ATV riders who will go down the trails afterward to pick them up. We'll cart our trash as far as we can, then swap out the bags for Richie when he runs out of energy," Rachel explained.

"That's genius," Mac said. "Will it hold me if I get tired?"

"Sure. We'll get Richie to pull your lazy butt though the woods."

"Or I could walk." Mac was dressed for the weather, from his brimmed khaki hat down to his waterproof hiking boots. His canvas jacket was covered in loops and pockets. Lori squinted. "Are those fishing lures?" she asked, pointing at a pair of silver hooks with feathered tufts hanging off one pocket flap.

He looked down and carefully patted his chest, stopping when he found them. "Probably. This is my fishing jacket. It's good for keeping the water off and blocking the wind."

She'd seen it in his boat the day she'd gone for a dip in Star Lake. "Big fisherman, are you?"

"It's my favorite thing," he agreed as they followed Rachel, Owen, and Richie past the tree line.

She already knew he liked to fish. Now she knew how much. Personally, she'd never held a rod in her life. To her, spending the day on the water meant suntan lotion, a book, and an air mattress in somebody's backyard pool.

But she was willing to try fishing. Even if she didn't like it, she figured an afternoon reading on a boat on the lake wouldn't be that much different from doing it on a floatie in a pool. All she needed was someone to invite her so she could try it.

The trails were a mess. Pop cans, candy bar wrappers, liquor bottles. The detritus of thoughtless hikers was endless. Even the pieces of trash coated with dust stood out among the bright new leaves and sprouts pushing through the bare soil. "I had no idea it would be this bad," she huffed as she stepped over a fallen log to snag a plastic grocery bag caught on a branch.

"Some of this is from snowmobilers over the winter. But a lot is just garbage already out here that is working its way to the surface," Rachel said as she tied their second garbage bag closed. They were only halfway through their portion of the trail. "We're cleaning up decades of carelessness. It's not going to happen overnight."

"How did you get involved with the Parks Committee?" Lori asked. She pushed back her hood, grateful the drizzle had stopped even if the sun hadn't yet made an appearance.

"Mac recruited me."

"How did Mac get involved?"

"He started the whole thing. But if you want details, you'll have to ask him."

Lori slowed to fall back in step with Mac. She and Rachel had been behind Richie as the little boy ran back and forth, grabbing whatever trash he'd been able to reach. They'd done a much more thorough job. Owen and Mac made up the third wave. "Want to trade walking buddies?" she asked Owen.

She fell into step beside Mac comfortably. "Rachel says you recruited her to the Holiday Beach Parks Committee. Why aren't you on it?"

"I stepped down last summer when I started construction on the house. I knew I wouldn't be able to commit fully, and I'm an all-or-nothing kind of guy."

"What got you involved in the first place?" She flashed her palm and stepped aside to grab a crumpled pop bottle from under a pile of leaves.

"Why do you ask?"

"I'm trying to brainstorm more ideas for *Modern Minnesota*. They've done pieces on community initiatives before. I'm wondering if this would be a good story for them. Will you tell me about it?"

"It's not a terrific story."

"Rachel says you started it?"

The sun decided to peek through a break in the clouds. Mac stripped off his coat and tied it around his waist. "Yeah, but it was for selfish reasons," he said.

"Now I have to know."

"A few years ago, when Doug was still a teenager, he bought his first snowmobile. It was a big deal because he'd just gotten his license. The second weekend he had it, he decided to take the trail around Star Lake with me as a passenger. He got about halfway around when we hit a bicycle that somebody abandoned on the path in the fall. It had been hidden under the snow. It threw him over the handlebar and tore his track to bits. We were lucky he wasn't seriously hurt."

"That's terrible! Were you okay?" She'd be surprised if the answer was yes. The man seemed to attract disasters.

"I went sideways. Fortunately, I missed the bike. But when spring came, I rounded up all the riders I knew and organized a trail cleanup."

"That's not a bad story."

Mac winced. "The snowmobile club we belonged to was supposed to be maintaining the trail. We'd pushed the cleanup for five years with one excuse or another. We weren't prepared for how badly the trails had deteriorated or how much they'd been abused. That first year, we pulled out several bikes, a bunch of tents, and a washing machine." He shook his head. "Still don't understand that one. Anyway, it was a mess. It took us four hard years to get it back into shape, including trimming back trees and pruning branches. Since then, we've just had to do regular annual maintenance."

Lori nodded along with his story, making notes in her head. "You said the town pays people to take care of it now?"

"They didn't at first. But when we were cleaning the trails, we identified more places that needed help, and it went beyond the scope of the snowmobile club. Since it was my big idea, they put me in charge, and we diversified into cleaning up the parks and the beaches."

"It sounds like the town should have been taking care of that," Lori said. All towns had maintenance budgets.

"The town was in bad shape back then. It was before we became Holiday Beach, the place where you went to celebrate the holidays. They could barely keep up. Volunteers got everything to a point where the town could maintain it again. We held fundraisers for new equipment to ease the burden on Holiday Beach's budget. Now that we have a solid tourist industry, the town's budget can afford summer students to help at the busy times, but the rest of the year, they depend on us."

They rounded a turn. The path before them widened, and the thick trees grew sparser, letting more sun shine through their branches. Small areas of grass appeared in patches. In the distance was the back of a brick building. "We did it!"

Rachel, Owen, and Richie waited for them at the edge of the clearing. Owen collected their garbage bags and consolidated them with his. "Seven full trash bags in a little more than two miles," he reported, shaking his head.

"It's not quite as bad as it sounds. We uncovered a tarp that had "Reunion 2010" on it that filled one bag all on its own, and a sleeping bag, still tied with a bungee, that went into another bag," Rachel said.

"That was a good afternoon's work," Lori said. She wished she'd stopped to take more pictures, but she'd been too busy talking to Mac. The second hour had flown by as she got to know him better.

He was right. It wasn't an inspiring story about trying

to make the whole planet a better place or about an invention that would provide clean energy for generations to come. But the core of his motivation was like the core of everything she'd learned about him. Mac wanted to do his part to make his little piece of the world a better place to live for himself and his neighbors. It wasn't a grand plan, but it was more relatable to a lot of people. That was something, and someone, she could get behind.

Mac dropped her off in the apartment building's parking lot. She got out of his truck but didn't close the door. With a week more of work to go, she decided to take a chance. "What would you say if I said at five-oh-one on Friday afternoon I'd like to buy you a drink and hear more about the Holiday Beach Parks Committee and how you got it up and running?" Lori asked.

"I wish you wouldn't."

"Oh." She didn't even have time to process her disappointment because he continued to speak.

"Because at five o'clock and thirty seconds, I'd like to offer to buy you a drink," Mac countered.

"Deal."

"But until then..."

Yes, until then. "You're my boss and you aren't going to take your arm out of that sling for fear of Dr. White," Lori said. Whatever she felt for Mac personally, she could lock it down tightly for a week while they worked together. They could be professional for five more days.

"Right," he agreed. "Especially that bit about Dr. White. You don't want to cross her. But Friday night?"

"It will be a date at five o'clock and one second." And she'd treasure it for the last weekend she was in town.

CHAPTER 18

NEVER HAD a week taken so long before. Doug and Lori had finished painting the exterior of the bowling alley just in time. The sun decided to get into summer mode with June right around the corner and increased its heat and brightness. Mac patted himself on the back for scheduling the larger exterior projects for earlier in the season. They'd all be grateful for more interior painting jobs over the next month, and that was all he had on the schedule.

Both active members of his team had pressed hard to finish their final contract and had loaded the van at half past four. They got to the office by ten to five. Mac handed them their paychecks. Doug hung around for a few minutes, then chuckled to himself. "Lori, we had a weird start, but it was a pleasure working with you. If Mac almost gets hit by lightning a second time, I hope we can work together again." Then he walked out the door, wishing them a good weekend.

The clock on the wall clicked hit five o'clock and Mac let out a huge sigh of relief. A month ago, he'd been looking for reasons to run Lori out of town. Now he was trying to come up with ways to get her to stay. This was his big chance to get some information on whether that was going to be possible. "Ms. Baker, your employment with Mackenzie Brothers Painting is officially over. Can I take you to dinner?"

"I'd like that."

"Can I pick you up in half an hour?" he asked.

She waved a paint-covered hand at him. "Better make it forty-five minutes."

Exactly three-quarters of an hour later, Lucy ran into him at the security door and let him into the building when he told her Lori had waved to him from her window. He knocked on her apartment door, and when she opened it, she took his breath away.

He'd only ever seen her dressed for work, either as a painter or as an architect-troublemaker next door to his house. This time, she was dressed for a date. She'd paired a white, yellow, and navy-striped blouse with a pair of navy capris and white sandals.

"Am I too early? Do you need a little more time?" he asked after she invited him in.

"No, I just need to grab my purse."

Mac could see her entire apartment from his spot at the front door. "You've already started packing," he noted. Not that she had much to start with. He'd seen the truck-load of furniture she arrived with. A futon, a stubby four-drawer dresser, a small table with ends that folded down, and two kitchen chairs. A small television sat on the dresser. A short row of books sat on the window ledge with a half-filled box beneath them. Three suitcases were stacked beside the futon with the top one acting as a coffee table. She had two more partially filled boxes on the counter by the sink, and a pile of collapsed boxes leaning against the cupboards. "How did you get all this in here?"

"I borrowed a friend's truck. When I got here, Lucy introduced me to Caleb, who helped me unload for twenty bucks."

"How are you going to get it all home? Where is home?" he asked. Doug knew more about her than he did.

"I'll take it home the same way, back to Minneapolis. I have an apartment over my grandmother's garage that's slightly larger than this place. I don't have to pay rent there, though. I'll move it all out on Monday or Tuesday since I have to be out by Wednesday." She stepped to the door. "I didn't ask. Where are we going?"

"I'm sure you've had takeout pizza from Colombo's, but have you eaten in the restaurant?" Holiday Beach had some nice restaurants. Colombo's was the place to go for anything Italian. It offered a little more intimacy than American Table or the Atlas Restaurant when it came to tables and lighting, so it had been Mac's first pick for a first date.

"I have not. I'm looking forward to it."

He took the scenic route to the restaurant. The streets were already clogged with out-of-towners coming out to open their cottages on the Memorial Day weekend for the season and campers eager to start the summer. It would be worse on Sunday when the town shut down certain roads in anticipation of the Memorial Day service.

They were still talking about the weekend's upcoming events when they were seated and the waiter took their wine orders. "I'll hang around for the Memorial Day service in the morning on Monday, and then take off with a full carload at lunchtime. I'll come back on Tuesday with the truck to get the rest," Lori said.

Mac nodded silently as he tried to figure out a way to help. "Tripp Turner from the Atlas Restaurant is going to give a speech at the eleven o'clock on behalf of retired military personnel in town and place a wreath at the war memorial by City Hall. I have breakfast tickets at his restaurant if you'd like to come with me. He does a fundraiser for a local VA hospital." There, that was something he could do for her, so she wasn't scrambling for a meal on her way out of town. Plus, it was another date, and another chance to see if they hit it off like he thought they would.

"Why do you have a spare? Were you already taking somebody?"

"You are much prettier company than Doug. He can get his own ticket," Mac joked.

"Then I'd love to."

They ordered their meals and suddenly Mac found his calendar full of plans for the weekend.

"Rachel said there's a sandcastle building contest on the beach on Saturday afternoon for the kids," Lori said between bites of butternut squash ravioli.

"There is."

"She also said there's an antique car show at the high school in the parking lot."

"It's huge. It's the first real chance collectors have to show off their vehicles after a Minnesota winter. We even have people from the city show up," he boasted.

"She also mentioned there are food trucks on Lakeside Drive in the evening and there's a band playing at the beach pavilion that evening," Lori continued.

"Apples and Oranges."

"Is that the name of a food truck? Is it vegetarian?"

"No, that's the name of the band. They're from Bixby. They play with great enthusiasm and are a local favorite."

"Mac, that sounds like code."

"It is. For not very good, but we support our own."

"It sounds like Holiday Beach kicks off summer with a bang this weekend."

"Oh, we do," he agreed. "Can I be the one to show you around?"

"I thought you'd never ask."

"When can I pick you up? Does three o'clock work? Or would you prefer later because it can be a long day?" Mac suggested. He almost said noon, but he was trying to be realistic for a second date, no matter how good this first one was going. He did have a few errands to run. If he hustled, he could get them all done in the morning, have a late lunch, and then enjoy the rest of the long weekend with Lori. If Saturday went well, they'd have two more days to spend together before she had to leave.

Lori gasped in delight as she took a bite of her fresh breadstick dipped in marinara sauce. "That sounds terrific. You may have to roll me to the beach if the rest of the food is like this. Why didn't you warn me, Mac?"

"It was a test. If you don't like the marinara, we can't date," he said. He was mostly joking.

Lori looked him dead in the eye as she hooked her finger over the lip of the sauce bowl and pulled it closer to her plate. "Mine."

"Okay, we can go out together."

"Only if you get your own bowl."

She was perfect.

CHAPTER 19

SHE HAD A MORE active social life in Holiday Beach than she'd ever had in the city. Lori packed the rest of her books and knickknacks into the single box she'd brought with her for her one-month stay. She'd made more friends and had more dates in four weeks than she'd had in the last four months. Of course, she wasn't spending half her time driving across the state to deal with the Parkmans anymore, but she wanted to give credit where credit was due, and that was to this town.

She'd made a poor impression before she'd even arrived, but Lori hoped she'd made inroads at improving it. Julie at Handler Hardware still hadn't completely warmed up to her, but Lori had been especially difficult in her quest to keep her unreasonable clients happy, so that was her own fault. Aside from that, her time in Holiday Beach had been more than she could have hoped for, especially considering the job had been more of a necessity than a choice.

With a paycheck in her pocket and new friends in her contact list, all she needed now was a job. Her one assignment was a good start, and her green communities idea had merit, but she needed more—a lot more—to make a living at it.

But that was a problem for another day. Lori had a long weekend stretched out in front of her and a good-looking guy to spend it with. She was going to make the most of the time she had left here.

It was too early for Mac to be knocking on her door. Lori was surprised to see Lucy standing in the hallway. "Come in," she offered.

Lucy took in all her boxes with a glance. "You're mostly packed already."

"It doesn't take long. I only had one truckful of stuff. The rest fit in my car."

"Is there anything I can do to get you to stay? You're the perfect tenant. You're leaving the suite in better shape than when you moved in."

"Unfortunately, no matter how good of a discount you give me, I still need a job to pay the rent. Holiday Beach is great, but it doesn't have an architecture firm in need of an associate." Which was a shame. She'd be happy designing garages and greenhouses if she got to put her names on the plans.

"We'll miss you. I stopped by for another reason too. There are a bunch of events going on today. I was wondering if you were going to check any of them out?" Lucy asked.

That's when Lori realized her landlady was dressed for a day in the sun. She smelled faintly of coconut, which made sense when Lori considered the sheen on her arms and legs was probably sunscreen. Lucy sported a ball cap with a pair of sunglasses perched on the brim, green walking shorts, a striped yellow-and-white tank top, and flip-flops. "Thanks, but I already have a date. Mac and I are going to hit the sandcastle building contest and the car show this afternoon."

"Roy and I are doing that too. We'll see you on the beach!"

Seeing Lucy's casual wear made her reassess her own wardrobe, but it was as good as it could be with her limited options. The suntan lotion was a good idea, though. Lori had barely finished slathering it on when there was another knock at her door. This time it was the one she'd been waiting for. "I'm ready," she said.

She'd never seen the streets of Holiday Beach so packed. "Is it always like this on a long weekend?" she asked Mac.

"Pretty much every weekend between now and Labor Day," he said, steering them around a gaggle of teenagers heading toward them, weighed down with ice cream cones and slushie drinks. "The weekdays are a little better until the end of June when school lets out. Then it's every local for themselves."

It was hectic, but Lori liked the buzz in the air. All the little shops that had been so quiet on her previous visits were buzzing, and various store-stamped bags paraded up and down the sidewalk on the arms of satisfied customers.

"Will there be room for us on the beach?"

"Lots. Don't worry." Mac took her hand and pulled her down an alley, which led to a back lane that eventually spilled them onto a residential street.

"This is much better," she said, revelling in the open space.

"And it will still take us right to the lake," Mac said. But he didn't let go of her hand, and she didn't pull it away.

Eighteen flags marked eighteen piles of sand along the edge of the beach. It looked like a backhoe had scooped a bucketful of sand from the beach and given each of the building teams a head start. They'd made the most of it. Dry moats circled tall towers dripping with gloppy streams of sand. Twigs and leaves stood proudly in the corners of the walls, protecting the castles within. The winning entry originally had a trio of bucket-castles, but two were crushed by a plastic dinosaur who was threatening the third. Lori had to agree with the points for originality.

She opted for an icy drink rather than an ice cream that would melt all over her hand before she had time to finish it. Mac did the same. "It's easier to carry," he said, as he led them down another side street to the high school parking lot, which was jammed with people and sparkling vehicles.

The classic convertibles were gorgeous and waxed to a high shine. But Lori made a beeline to a vehicle she'd only ever seen on late-night repeats. "Is that what I think it is?"

Mac laughed. "It is. It's one of the most popular vehicles every single year. Want to meet the owner of this authentic Korean War-era Army ambulance?"

All she could do was nod. Her grandma was an ardent fan of *M*A*S*H*, even though it had been off the air for longer than Lori had been alive. She'd seen more than her share of re-runs playing while she was visiting as a kid, and even now, she recognized the theme song when it came on in the background.

"Adam Wayne, this is my friend Lori. Watch the keys. I think she's ready to run away with your beautiful Bessie," Mac said.

The man with pure white hair offered her a calloused hand. "It's always nice to meet someone who appreciates my Bessie."

"She's a beauty. My grandma would go nuts if she was here." The thin mattress and the small metal first aid kit clipped to the wall of the ambulance spoke to medicine of a different era. The owner even let her climb in so Mac could take a picture of her, which she promptly texted to her grandma.

She returned the favor when Mac found himself behind the wheel of a Model A, the oldest vehicle in the show. Lori didn't have an in-depth knowledge of cars and trucks, but she could appreciate other people's passions.

They were closer to her apartment than the beach when they finished their tour of the parking lot, so Lori invited Mac in for a drink. All she could offer was a glass of water or a can of diet cola. Other than that, her fridge was empty. But she had two chairs and air conditioning.

"This summer is going to be a scorcher if this weather is any indication of what's to come," Mac said as he refilled his glass at the sink.

"That's going to make your job difficult."

"It's better than rain."

"True."

"This was a good idea. Now we can cool off before round two."

"Food trucks and a band, right?" she confirmed. It wasn't a typical dinner-and-dancing date, but it sounded like a lot of fun. It wasn't something she'd ever get in the city. She added another note to the list of things she was going to miss about Holiday Beach.

"The best food trucks in the state," he promised.

"I haven't had a chance to ask, but what did you

decide to do about your staircase banister?" Lori asked. "The glass would have been gorgeous, but if it's not an option in your timeframe, what are you going to do?"

"This really smart woman I know suggested a slat wall. I've done some research of my own and it turns out she's right. It'll be perfect."

"It will be. What are you going to make it out of?"

"That's to be determined, but I'm leaning toward a whitewashed poplar," Mac said. "I don't want more pine. It'll turn the room too yellow."

She hadn't considered that option, but if anybody knew about color, it would be a professional painter. "You won't regret it. Your house is going to be great, Mac."

"It's nothing as fancy as what you designed next door, but it's all I need."

Was there a pang of regret in his words? She couldn't understand why. "Mac, what's happening next door was specifically reimagined to be a summer property used primarily to entertain. I can hardly recognize what it started as, but it was a lot closer to your place than you know. You're building a home to be loved and lived in. You really should take Kurt Crabb up on his offer to visit once you're done." If she ever got to design a place for herself, it would be a cross between her magazine-nominated design—the original—and Mac's place. No solariums or pool houses for her. Just lots of space and light and comfort.

"He was probably just being polite."

"He's the senior editor of *Modern Minnesota* and he's on the boards of tons of organizations, including the one that ran the contest I won. He doesn't have time to waste being polite. He meant it. Promise me you'll call him."

Now he was smiling again. "Okay. I promise."

"Have you decided on color for the upstairs bedrooms?" she asked. The walls were up, but everything was still raw. She didn't know when she'd be back in town to see the finished product, but she wanted to hear everything while she could.

Their bathroom wallpaper debate ended at the same time as they ran out of drinks. It was six o'clock, and the worst heat of the day was over. Lori grabbed her jacket on the way out and they headed back to the beach, stopping at Mac's truck so he could grab his. "The streets are less crowded," she commented.

"A lot of folks will go home for supper and anybody with kids is done for the day," he said. "This evening is more for teens and adults than little ones."

The Fry Guys truck had a line ten people deep, so they diverted to Tito's Taqueria.

"I think I need this truck to follow me around," Lori said, licking her fingers before reluctantly accepting the napkin Mac offered.

"It's no good. I tried to bribe them to come to my jobsites, but they insist on being at the beach where the customers are. I promised to provide equivalent sales, but they still said no."

"That's no way to run a business," she commiserated.

"I don't know. Making their customers come to them saves them gas money," Mac acknowledged.

"If only your customers could bring their houses to you to paint."

He sighed dramatically. "If only. We have a job in Bemidji next week. We're going to be driving for hours."

"That puts us even farther apart. If you have a job south, closer to Minneapolis, tell me. Maybe I can meet you for lunch if I can get away from the office. Or supper after work," she suggested. "It wouldn't be a proper date but..."

"I'll take what time I can get with you too," Mac agreed.

Things had been going well, but that was a huge step. She was willing to take it, but Mac had beaten her to the words. "Are we really going to do this? I mean, we've only known each other for a month."

"That's not true," Mac interrupted. "We've known each other for months. We've only liked each other for a few weeks. I think we've got a shot at something here. Unless you start developing the land on the other side of my cabin. Or across the street. Or anything within tree-falling distance."

She laughed. "Okay, that's fair. But I can still tell you that wallpaper should only be in a powder room and not a full four-piece bathroom, right?"

"You can tell me, but I'm still hanging the wallpaper."

"I see I still have a lot of work to do," she teased.

All the picnic tables and benches at the beach were occupied, so they found a patch of grass to sit on and watched the sun begin to set over the lake. "I've been thinking. Instead of you having to make two trips, why don't we load the truck on Monday afternoon? Doug can drive the truck and you and I can take your car so we can do it in one trip."

"That's a lot of extra work for you and your brother," Lori said, although she loved the idea. It gave them more time together. She'd get to spend the drive with Mac and would even get to introduce him to her grandma.

"Doug needed to go to Minneapolis, anyway. He can do his thing while we have an early supper, and then I'll drive back with him that evening."

"I'd like to say no, but honestly, I'd really appreciate it."

"Then consider it done."

Streetlights and strings of bulbs hung around the large gazebo sprang to life before the sun was down. A five-piece band filled the enclosed platform and soon, mostly recognizable pop and country songs filled the air.

The open grassy space between the gazebo and the start of the sandy beach filled with couples doing their best to dance along with the music. Mostly, it was a lot of swaying and laughing, which suited Lori just fine.

"You were honest about the band," she said. They hadn't been terrific, but the crowd had a great time. Now Mac was walking her home, holding her hand again. A cool breeze blew off the water, making her grateful for her jacket.

"Like I said, they play with great enthusiasm."

He walked her all the way to her building door. "What are you doing tomorrow?"

"Nothing much. More packing." She only had a few things left to throw in a box, and now that Mac had offered the use of his truck, she didn't have to worry about the rest. She should probably send out more emails even though it was a long weekend, but she couldn't work up the desire to think of work after such a pleasant day. "How about you?"

"I thought I might spend a nice day on the lake. How do you feel about fishing?"

She didn't have strong feelings about fish one way or another. But spending a Sunday on Star Lake sounded like heaven. "I'm willing to give it a try."

"The fish bite early, though. Would you be able to meet me at the marina at seven o'clock?"

"In the morning? Of a long weekend? I must really like you, Mac."

He leaned closer. "Good, because I really like you too. I like you enough to kiss you good night."

"You know, I lost my job after my clients destroyed part of your house and I saved you after you were almost hit by lightning. I think the least I deserve is a good-night kiss after a great date like today," she said.

"I think so too."

His lips were a little rough, like he spent a lot of time outside in the sun and wind. But they were gentle too, and he pulled back much too soon. "Now I'll have sweet dreams."

"Me too."

CHAPTER 20

Seventy-two more hours until he was free of the sling. Mac had begun referring to it as his own personal albatross. All he wanted to do was stretch and be able to use his right arm again. He could cast lefthanded, but he wasn't nearly as good at it. It would also be nice to be able to hold Lori's hand in either of his, instead of having to ensure she only walked on his left side.

And speaking of Lori, being able to hug her was high on his list of things to do. But it wouldn't be today. He'd barely be able to manage his boat. But he'd have good company.

He'd seen her reaction when he invited her to come fishing with him. The fish weren't going to be the point; it was spending time with her. She got that. The seven o'clock timeline had caused her small hesitation, so Mac took steps to make it worth her while.

He loaded two thermoses full of piping hot coffee into his backpack and a handful of sugar packets, along with a container stuffed to the brim with sweet buns and treats from By the Cup's bakery counter. Now that the summer season was upon the town, Rachel had begun getting daily deliveries from Butterlicious Bakery to keep up with the tourists' demands. The first people through the door got the biggest selection, and he'd been the third in line when the coffee shop opened. He added a couple of bottles of water for later in the morning and a handful of napkins. It wasn't eggs Benedict and mimosas, but it wasn't a half-bad alternative.

Lori was waiting at the edge of the pier when he arrived. She was holding the gate open for a steady stream of boaters and folks carrying fishing gear who were also out for a good morning on the lake. "I didn't expect seven to be rush hour around here."

"It's the tail end of rush hour," he said. "The real early birds were out here at six."

"Thanks for letting me sleep in then," she said.

"I brought you coffee to make up for it. Sugars are in the bag."

"My hero. I already packed my coffeepot."

It took them a minute to settle into his boat. Mac stowed their breakfast under a seat, then took his position beside the motor while Lori braced herself to work the pull cord. "Now I know why you invited me," she said as she grabbed the handle.

"Honestly, this is just a bonus. I could have gotten one of the guys on the dock to help me."

"You bought me coffee. It's the least I can do."

The motor caught on the second pull. Mac quickly backed them out of his slip and headed to open water. "Let's see if my favorite spot is taken yet." A couple of years earlier, he'd found a submerged log at the entrance to a small bay about a twenty-minute ride north of the marina. It never failed to have something willing to take the bait early in the morning. Even better, it offered a great view of the lake as the sun cleared the trees and got on with its day.

His spot was open, so he lowered the anchor—a cinderblock on a chain—gently into the water to avoid scaring away any nearby fish.

"Food or fishing rod first?" Lori asked.

"Food," was his definitive answer. Not just because Lori would appreciate it and he wanted to enjoy another meal with her, but it would also give the fish time to find the shadow of the boat. He could multitask with two of his favorite pastimes.

A thin steam rose from his coffee. They drank in silence, listening to the not-quite silence of the woods and the occasional boat motor in the distance. "Okay, this is pretty nice," Lori said.

"But?"

"But nothing. It's nice. I'm not used to it. I'm listening for car horns and sirens and jets coming in for a landing, not rustling leaves and birds. It's an adjustment."

He could understand that. For him, there was no comparison, but it took time to acclimate to new surroundings. "You're also probably more at home on a jobsite."

"With power tools and banging and instructions being shouted and a radio playing in the background? Yeah, I like that kind of noise too," Lori agreed.

"Sports or music on the radio?" he asked.

"Either, so long as it's not talk radio or a murder podcast."

"What? No serial-killer podcasts?"

"No! Unless it has Steve Martin or Martin Short, I'm not interested. I'm strangely addicted to science podcasts, though, but I prefer to listen to them at home," she admitted. Then she got distracted by caramel dripping off her cinnamon bun and onto the metal seat that stretched across the boat.

"Just rinse it off with lake water when you're done eating."

"I can't splash water onto the seat. It'll ruin it."

"Lori, it's a boat. It's made to withstand a little water, I promise." Mac laughed.

The coffee and pastries were very civilized. His attempts to cast were less so. Casting lefthanded was challenging enough, but the added pressure of having Lori watch was giving him the worst case of fumble fingers he'd ever had.

He dropped his hook the first time he grabbed it. The second time, he pricked his finger. Then he got the line caught under his seat as he twisted in the boat to give himself room to cast and he smacked himself in the head with his rod.

His grumbles turned to laughter when she muttered, "Fishing is super relaxing, Lori. Honest."

"Do you want to try?"

"What will you do when I catch a fish?" she asked.

"Probably quit forever."

"Then I'd better not. For your ego's sake."

He didn't stay out as long as he usually did, not wanting Lori to get bored. They finished their coffees and breakfast pastries, and he regaled her with a couple of fish tales of successful trips where he caught more than the branches he'd hooked that morning.

"Would you have been able to reel in anything if you had gotten a bite this morning?" she asked. "I know your arm is better, but..."

"Let's just say the fish would have had a better than normal chance to escape." He looked at her and grinned. "Besides, like Zane Grey said, 'If I fished only to capture fish, my fishing trips would have ended long ago.' I didn't come out with you this morning just for the trout."

"Wait. Zane Grey, the old western writer?"

"He was multifaceted."

"A fishing cowboy. I'm impressed. Do you read westerns?"

"I have a couple of his books. Mostly because of that quote. But I'm not a big reader. Are you?" He'd seen that a box of books had been among her meager possessions in her apartment. If they were important enough for her to bring, she must have an entire library back in Minneapolis.

"I read more in the winter. If the weather's good, I'd rather be outside. Especially at a baseball game."

"Do you see the Twins often?"

"Not as often as I'd like." Lori beamed at the topic. "I try to get tickets a couple of times a year. The smaller, independent leagues are a lot more affordable for an associate and just as much fun."

"Baseball, huh?"

"Always. Maybe I can take you to a game this summer. To say thanks for exposing me to fishing."

"That'll be a date." A day in the sun at a baseball diamond wouldn't be that different from a day in the sun on the lake.

The boat puttered into his slip, and he jumped out to tie the lines before helping Lori onto the dock. Castor Marina was bustling now, with water-skiers and wake-boarders getting ready for a day on the water.

"This place is hopping," Lori said. She stepped to the

side to let a horde of kids in life vests, herded by a flustered mom in her own vest, waddle by like penguins.

"You have to get up early to get the fish before the other boats scare them off."

"I'm sorry you didn't get out as early as you wanted."

"Don't apologize. I had a great morning." He hesitated. "What are your plans for the rest of the day?" They hadn't formalized anything until lunch the following day. He didn't know what they could do, but he was certain they could think of something.

"Emily and I are doing pre-summer mani-pedis at her house this afternoon. I think Gloria is going to join us."

He'd been too slow. "That sounds like fun. You've made a few friends during your stay."

"I've worked hard to mend fences, but it's been easiest with people I didn't meet during my work time in Holiday Beach. I think Julie Handler's almost ready to forgive me after all the stress I caused her and her hardware store."

"You were pretty hard on her. Give her time. I think it's helping that the project manager the Parkmans have now was so rude he was banned."

Lori gasped. "That's some juicy gossip. I haven't heard a word about the house since I left. I thought everyone was avoiding the subject around me."

"We were trying to be polite, but that build has stopped dead. I even saw Aaron Gillespie over there in his official capacity the other day."

"Why would they need to call the sheriff?"

"I didn't ask."

She snickered at the wink he gave her. "You mean you'll hear about it from somebody else," she translated.

"It's a small town," Mac said with a shrug. But they both laughed.

He offered to drive her to Emily's if she gave him directions, but Lori turned him down. It was good she had other friends in Holiday Beach, he told himself. It gave her more reasons to visit. "Are we still on for tomorrow?" he asked.

"I hope so. Would you like to come to the service at the war memorial with me?"

"I wouldn't miss it. We'll do that, then lunch, and then drive you back to Minneapolis," he said.

Lori nodded. "That sounds like a good plan. I'm sorry to be wasting half a day of your long weekend, though."

"You are time well spent. If I could have thought of a way to keep you in Holiday Beach longer, I would have." He had a plan and people to talk to, but it was nothing he could put together in less than a month. By the time he got all the pieces in place, she'd probably have another job, anyway.

"Well, I suppose you could get almost hit by lightning again and put your other arm in a sling, but that seems a little extreme when we could just see each other on weekends."

Mac flinched. "Yes, let's stick to weekends. And tomorrow."

"And definitely tomorrow."

CHAPTER 21

"DID HE KISS YOU GOODBYE?" Emily asked, her brown eyes wide in anticipation.

"I'm not telling," Lori said.

"That's a yes!" Gloria gave a whoop. "I knew I saw a spark when you two were flirting while he was hanging upside down from the Escape Room's roof."

The three women sat in Emily's living room. The patio door to her balcony was open, and a warm summer breeze blew through the room, drying the nail polish on their toes. Lori had gotten to know Emily through their shared love of medical dramas. She only knew Gloria from the hotel, but Gloria knew Emily quite well since they worked next door to each other. With everybody having a rare Saturday afternoon off over a long weekend, they'd decided to pamper themselves while they enjoyed the weather. As soon as their feet were done, they were putting on flip-flops and heading out for a walk on the boardwalk along the beach.

"I was not flirting with him! We didn't even like each other then. I was just being a good Samaritan."

"But you flirted later," Emily added.

"Only once I stopped working for him," Lori agreed. "I wasn't going to cause problems at two jobs in a row."

"Speaking of jobs, what are you going to do back in Minneapolis?" Gloria asked.

"Network until my feet are sore and I wear off this pedicure," Lori said. "It's never a good time to go job hunting, but hopefully the article I'm doing for *Modern Minnesota* and the interior paint and design work I did for Mackenzie Brothers will add some interest to my job history." She was trying to keep a positive attitude, but it was difficult.

"Paint and design work?" Gloria parroted.

"I made a couple of suggestions to a client for designs, and she was very appreciative and named me in her online review. Doug and Mac liked it and said they'd mention it if they were called as references, as long as I promised to do a little long-distance consulting for the rest of the summer." It wasn't part of her degree she often used, but Lori had studied the basics of interior design. It had been a fun exercise to stretch those old brain muscles, and Mrs. Pham had been very grateful.

"Flexibility is a good thing to show a prospective employer," Emily agreed. "Multitasking, multi-talented people are easier to place."

Lori pinched her lips together in confusion at Emily's tone. "What was that?"

"What was what?"

"You said, "Multitasking, multi-talented people are easier to place." You sound like a head-hunter for one of those recruitment companies."

"Maybe I am. That's a line from the commercial I booked for Career Finder!"

Flip-flops and cotton balls went flying as the women jumped to their feet. "You got a job?" Lori shrieked. "An acting job?"

"Why didn't you say something? We should be celebrating!" Gloria added.

"Yeah, this is huge news. My friend is going to be on television."

Emily fanned her face. Lori couldn't see a blush on her dark cheeks, but Emily's eyes shone with unshed tears. "I can't believe it. I got a commercial. I'm going to Minneapolis next Thursday to film it. Roy shifted my schedule to give me three days off."

"You can stay with me. I have a bed back home, and you're welcome to use the futon." It would be a small thank-you to the first friend Lori had made in Holiday Beach.

"That would be amazing. Thank you."

"You'll have to let us know when it airs so we can have a watch party," Gloria said.

"For a commercial?"

"Why not?" Gloria asked.

"I'll watch with you, even if it's through a video chat," Lori promised.

Once their toes were dry, the trio celebrated Emily's news with a round of milkshakes and camped out under a tree to watch the various activities happening on the beach. Brave blue kids in the water for their first swims of the season. Two groups of teens played volleyball on one of the courts in the corner of the park. The rest of the folks were enjoying lunches from the food trucks or picnicking with food they'd brought from nearby restaurants.

"I am going to miss this place so much."

"It only gets better as we get into the summer. You have to come back for Independence Day. Our fireworks display is the second-best in the state," Emily bragged.

"Second best?" Lori asked.

"We don't have the budget that Minneapolis does," Emily explained. "But we put on a spectacular show."

"I'll have to book a room."

Gloria snorted and raised a hand to her mouth. "Good luck with that. We've been booked solid for months. Besides, why pay for a room when you can just stay with one of us?"

"Are you sure?"

"You can stay with me. It'll be payback for next week. Maybe we can get a roommate exchange deal going for you coming to visit Mac and me getting future auditions," Emily suggested.

"That's a deal."

CHAPTER 22

MAC COULD MANAGE A NAIL GUN, even with his arm in a sling, but he did better on the chop saw. He cut the final piece, then passed it to Doug, who sanded the edges and added it to the pile.

"Is that it?" his brother asked.

"All that's left is the assembly."

"After lunch?"

Mac's stomach growled his answer. After he'd said goodbye to Lori, he went home to find Doug hard at work on the boards he ordered to make the slat wall for his staircase. "It's one of the last things that needs to be done downstairs," Doug had told him. "Everything else is drywalled and painted. All you need now is for your kitchen cabinets to arrive and the countertops to be measured and delivered. Aside from that, you could live down here comfortably in the guest room and bath until you get the upstairs finished."

After a lot of evenings and another weekend, his open concept main floor was almost completed. His friends had helped put up and patch his walls and ceiling. After that, it hadn't taken him and Doug long to prime and paint the massive empty room. Since he hadn't been able to work on the jobsite, it had been easy enough to book the flooring guys, electricians, and plumbers to come to him. All the contractors around Holiday Beach knew each other, so they were happy to work Mac's jobs into odd holes in their schedules. Before he knew it, the main floor was almost done.

His primary suite upstairs was much nicer than the main floor guest room, but the guest room had the benefit of being completed. Now that Mac was returning to work and his friends had summer weather and vacations to enjoy, the rest would take a lot longer. But Doug was right. He could comfortably live downstairs for months.

"When are the cupboards coming?" Doug asked.

"Next week."

"You'll be able to cook again."

They looked at each other and laughed. "Okay, you'll still make all your meals on the barbecue, but you'll have the option if you suddenly get struck by the desire to bake a batch of brownies," Doug said.

They looked at each other again. "Mmm, brownies," they said in unison.

They abandoned their project for lunch, which consisted of a drive into town for meatball subs and a stop at Butterlicious Bakery for brownies.

"You know, this is a big place for a single guy," Doug said as he waited for Mac to flip over the board he was staining. It was the final preparation stage before they assembled the slat wall.

His baby brother was anything but subtle. "It is. It would be less big for two. Or exactly the right size for two adults and a couple of minis." That had been the plan. It had taken longer than he'd liked to start construction, but it wasn't too late. He could happily spend the rest of his days in this house, but he'd be happier doing it with the right company.

"I'm looking forward to seeing how you and Lori turn out as a couple."

"Why? We get along fine."

"You also fight like cats and dogs when you're on opposite sides of an issue. When she's back in Minneapolis, this weekend honeymoon is going to be over."

"Maybe, but it's going to be a lot of fun while it lasts." There was no reason it couldn't last for a very long time.

"Besides, you aren't getting any younger, Bobby."

"I'm only thirty-three," Mac protested. "I have my own business—"

"Shared business," Doug interrupted.

"Business," Mac repeated. "I own my own home. I'm relatively good-looking, grill a mean steak, and can sit through an entire Christmas movie with only two groans. I'm a catch."

"A catch without a safe staircase."

"Then keep painting and help get your brother set up."

They worked in silence until Doug said, "I wonder if Lori can bake brownies."

CHAPTER 23

THE AMERICAN FLAG waved in the breeze, the red and white stripes flashing against the clear blue sky. Tripp Turner had spoken eloquently about his time in the military and about the men and women he'd worked with and the legacy they carried from those who had worn the uniforms before them. There was a solemn moment at the end before people broke away to reflect in their own ways. Mac and Lori spoke to Tripp for a moment, but a lot of folks wanted to speak to the veteran about his service.

"It seems our lunch has turned into a goodbye party," Mac said after they had left to have lunch. Roy, Lucy, Doug, Emily, Rachel, and Caleb, who she'd met during that afternoon at Mac's place, had staked out a place in the park for a picnic. It was nothing fancy, just cold-cut sandwiches and canned drinks.

"Why is it that everything immediately tastes twice as good when you eat it outside?" Lori wondered out loud.

"Being outside also makes you twice as hungry," Lucy added.

"That's true. Can you pass the salt-and-vinegar chips, please?"

The weather was cooperating, but the forecast said it was supposed to rain that afternoon, cutting the weekend short by a few hours. Lori had already noticed an exodus of cars and trucks heading out of town. The ones towing trailers and campers left first. The rest were lingering at the beach, even as the clouds rolled in.

"We had a great start to the tourist season," Rachel said. "I think it's going to be even busier than last year. Owen is gloating."

"Why?" Roy asked as he tried to steal a potato chip from Lucy.

"His grandfather told him he'd bought too much stock over the winter. Owen said they'd need it. Owen was right. They're planning to close tomorrow morning to give themselves a chance to restock all the shelves. This week-end's tourists cleaned out all the antique furniture they had on display. One weird woman bought every bell they had in the store. All of them," Rachel repeated, mystified.

"Mickey says the hotel is fully booked from the end of June through the Labor Day weekend," Roy said. The dark-haired man made another try for his fiancée's chips. "I'm going to have to hire more bar staff too. It's nice to be busy again."

For a brief second, Lori thought about applying to work as a waitress at the Escape Room. But that wasn't a real solution to her problem. She needed patience to find the right job. Patience and luck.

"We should get going," Mac said. "We'll make it to Minneapolis late this afternoon, but I don't want to drive home too late at night."

Lori didn't want to leave, but she was anxious to get

going. If one month in Holiday Beach had turned her life around this much, the next month in the city had to have even more in store for her. Although it was going to be hard to top a new boyfriend. "This is a great way to end my month here. Emily has already offered me a place to stay for the Independence Day weekend, so I'll get to see you all again soon."

"We'll see you then. Thanks for the great job you did painting your apartment. I'll be happy to be a reference if you need one," Lucy offered.

"Thank you. I may take you up on that." Living above her grandmother's garage was always supposed to be temporary. It was another thing she had to add to her to-do list, but that wouldn't happen until she had a job.

It didn't take long to load her belongings into the back of Mac's truck. They covered everything with a tarp and tucked into the corners. "We should be okay if we stay ahead of the storm," Doug said.

Lori gave him the address, which he entered into his GPS. "I'll stop for gas and see you there," he said, leaving her alone with Mac.

"I can't believe this is goodbye already."

"We have four more hours."

"Then let's make them count."

Mac was an excellent road trip partner. They found an afternoon baseball game on the radio, stopped at By the Cup for coffees for the road, and brainstormed positions to apply for during the three-hour ride to Minneapolis.

"If architecture firms contract with structural engineers, why shouldn't an architect apply to a structural engineer's office?" he asked. "I've worked with enough of them to know some of the fixes they suggest are downright ugly. I'll bet their clients would love to have someone like you on staff."

It was an intriguing idea, but a long shot at best. Since it would cost her nothing but time, though, there was no reason not to invest a couple of hours in some unlikely emails. "I'll think about it."

"The worst they can say is no."

"You say that like it's not a problem," Lori said. Heaven knew she'd heard that word often enough over the last month to know it didn't get any easier.

"I wish I could make it easier for you."

"Every no gets me closer to a yes. At least that's what my grandma tells me."

"I can't wait to meet her."

"Me either." Not that she had a choice. After hearing about how she'd gone head-to-head with the man next door when she worked for the Parkmans and how she saved him and ended up working for him, her grandma insisted on an introduction under the threat of turning off the hot water heater.

The introduction did not go as planned.

"Grandma, this is Bob Mackenzie, but he goes by Mac. Mac, this is my grandmother, Arlene Baker."

"Ma'am." Mac stepped forward, his hand outstretched.

Her grandmother waited. Deliberately. She gave Mac a hard once-over and then slowly shook his hand. "Bob."

Lori blinked. Her grandmother was never rude like this. It was a Baker point of pride to have impeccable manners. "Grandma!"

Mac soldiered on with a smile on his face. "It's nice to meet you. Lori has spoken about you a lot."

"She's mentioned you too. That her boss asked her on a date."

"No, Grandma, I specifically told you we didn't go out until after my contract had expired. Nobody took advantage of anybody."

His smile faltered. "Why don't I start unloading your car?" Mac asked. He excused himself with a nod, leaving Lori alone with the woman she'd thought would be excited to meet her boyfriend.

"Grandma, what was that?"

"It was bad enough when you told me about your new job. Lori, Bakers hire house painters. We don't work for them. We certainly don't date them. What are you thinking?"

"I was thinking a smart, handsome man with his own business who thinks I'm smart and talented asked me out after ensuring there was no conflict of interest." Mac had more going for him than her last two boyfriends combined. Lori didn't know how her grandmother didn't see it. "Since when is working for a living beneath a Baker?"

"You went to college to be an architect. Can you really picture yourself being happy with somebody whose dinner conversation is paint colors?"

Lori's eyes burned. "I always took being a Baker and living up to the family's standards as a serious responsibility. But if the family's standards include being rude to people who have done absolutely nothing to offend you, I have some serious thinking to do. Mac and I will unpack my car, and his brother will be here any minute with the rest of my things. Since he's a partner in the same family company, I'll spare you the embarrassment of shaking his hand."

"Lori—"

She didn't look back. Lori hefted her box of books onto her hip and strode through the open garage door to the staircase on the exterior of the building. She still couldn't believe how rude her grandmother had been to Mac. The Bakers were proud, not prejudiced. At least, not that she'd ever noticed before today's disastrous afternoon.

"Mac, I apologize for my grandma. That was wrong and rude of her."

"I appreciate you setting her straight about me not dating my staff. That rumor would be hard to disprove if it started making the rounds." He looked a little shaken as he replied.

"I think you're a catch. At least, that's what your brother called you." When he offered her a small smile, she pulled him into a hug. "I told him you were much better than a fish."

She sighed in relief when he hugged her back. "Thanks for that."

The two of them only needed to make three trips to empty her car. She pulled to the side so she didn't block the garage door on her grandmother, then offered Mac a class of water. "I'll go grocery shopping tonight," she told him.

"Microwave breakfast quiches and fish sticks?"

"Did you snoop in my apartment's freezer?" she demanded. "And it's not that bad. I have lots of veggies with my fish sticks."

"It's not great."

"I have an oven here. I'll make you a real supper sometime. Something that requires an oven," Lori promised. She could cook a pizza in her oven. If she bought the pizza that came with a pan. There was nothing wrong with frozen meals.

She gave Mac a tour, which lasted all of two minutes and three rooms. Her bedroom with her bed and its memory-foam mattress she'd missed desperately, her three-piece bathroom which was smaller than the one she'd just left and lacked a bathtub, and the main room with its kitchen, island, and the living room.

It looked worse than she remembered.

"How long have you lived here?" Mac asked.

"I was here for a couple of months before I moved to Holiday Beach. My apartment building was sold. They converted it into condos. I'd hoped to buy it, but I got outbid."

"That's hard. It took me forever to find the right piece of property to build on, and even then, it was a lot of work to get into shape," Mac commiserated. "At least you have this place to fall back on."

"Yeah, that's lucky. I don't think I could find another Lucy in the city to cut me a sweet deal, even if I did offer to paint."

A rumble of thunder drew their attention to the window. The clouds they'd stayed ahead of for the drive from Holiday Beach had caught up to them. Fortunately for her, so had Doug with her load of furniture.

"We should get moving," Mac said.

He was relegated to boxes and small appliances since he was still working with one arm. Lori and Doug got her futon, mattress, and dresser inside before the rain started. Her television got a little wet, but the raindrops on the plastic case wiped right off. She and Doug both were briefly caught in a downpour as they raced up the stairs with a final chair apiece.

"And I'm home," Lori said as she collapsed onto the futon.

Doug looked around her apartment. "It's bigger than your last place." When Mac coughed, he smiled. "I had hoped to hang around town today, but the weather reports say this storm is going to get worse later in the evening, so I think we should head out earlier than we initially planned. What do you say—should I run out and grab some dinner to eat on the drive back?" he asked Mac.

"I'd appreciate it."

"There are four fast-food restaurants in a strip a few blocks from here." Lori gave him directions, and Doug darted back into the rain.

"At least he gave us a few minutes to say goodbye in private," Mac said.

"Part of me wishes he doesn't come back so I can keep you here," Lori whispered.

"Hey, it's not forever. It's for a week. Maybe two." Mac pulled her closer with his good arm. "And the next time I see you, I'll be able to give you a proper hug. That's definitely something to look forward to."

She snuggled deeper into his chest. "A century ago, we would have been stuck with letters. I hope you realize I expect to video chat with you every day." Seeing him would be almost as good as being there. "And I expect you to show me everything you do to your house. I can't wait to see what the staircase is going to look like."

"I may purposely not show you just so you have to come out to see it."

There was no avoiding the next conversation. "I'm going to be hitting the pavement hard for the next week or two, applying to a bunch of engineering firms like my boyfriend suggested. I may not be able to make it back to Holiday Beach for a couple of weekends."

"I know you're coming out for Independence Day. How about if I promise to come either next weekend or the one after that for certain?" Mac offered. "I come to you, and you see if there's a baseball game we can go to on the weekend."

She squeezed tighter. "Best. Boyfriend. Ever!"

Lori kissed him goodbye. Then Mac kissed her goodbye. And then she went to give Mac a thank you kiss for her goodbye kiss, but they were interrupted by a truck honking in the driveway. "Your brother is entirely too efficient," Lori complained.

"He is, but he's starting the workday alone tomorrow so I can get my sling off, so I'd better go." Mac cupped her chin with his good hand. "You are going to knock all those emails and future interviews out of the park. I expect daily updates, okay?"

"I will if you will."

He grinned. "Deal. Should we seal it with a kiss?"

Another honk sounded from below.

Lori laughed. "Next time."

CHAPTER 24

It was Lori's fault. First, everything went wrong because she was there. Now everything was going wrong because she wasn't.

Mac pulled his T-shirt over his head and threw it into the washing machine. The only benefit of wearing a black shirt was that it would hide the coffee stains. He texted Doug to let him know he'd be even later to the jobsite than he'd predicted, then spent the next ten minutes hunting down a clean T-shirt.

Monday night had been okay. He and Doug had gotten home late, but he'd fallen asleep before midnight. Tuesday morning rolled around much too early, and he'd dragged himself to Dr. White's office. That's when the problems started. She was an hour late, and he was the third appointment of the day. When he finally got in to see her, the news was shocking.

"This isn't good, Doctor. I'm tired from doing the exercises you showed me. How am I supposed to put in a full day of work after this?" Mac had demanded. He had full range of motion in his shoulder, but it felt like it he'd been painting for twelve hours straight.

"It's going to take time, Bob. Give yourself a break. You haven't used it for a month." She pressed her fingertips into her own shoulder and raised her elbow. "This movement uses a lot more muscles and tendons than you realize. Do not, and I repeat not because I know you don't listen, overdo it this week. Take breaks. You can take an over-the-counter painkiller if you have to, but try to stick to ice packs and hot showers. It'll take some time to get back to where you were. You aren't as young as you used to be," she said.

"Now you're just being mean."

Since he was already late, he headed home to change into his work clothes. That was when his quick cup of coffee turned into another big delay. Luckily for him, the cottage they were painting was nearby. Unfortunately, the owners were neighbors of the Parkmans and had taken lessons from them in how to treat contractors.

His brother's usually calm brown eyes had narrowed to slits. That was never a good sign. "Mac, I'm glad you're here. Mr. Dempsey has requested some last-minute changes."

"I'm sure it won't be a problem."

He was wrong. Again. The changes Neil wanted would put them days behind on their schedule. It was already going to be hard to keep to their timeline since his arm was not as good as he anticipated. It took several calls and a bribe for Rachel to let Caleb switch some shifts before Mac was able to confirm they'd be able to meet the Dempseys' new requests.

He stumbled into his house and the thankfully

finished downstairs shower two hours after their usual quitting time. He'd done his best to follow Dr. White's advice, but his shoulder was killing him. Painkillers and hot water took the edge off. It had been more than twenty-four hours since he'd last spoken to Lori. It felt like a lifetime.

"I love you, sofa," Mac whispered as he fell into his recliner. He hit Lori's contact button, leaned the phone against a can of primer, and relaxed into the cushions.

Her face appeared on his screen after two rings. "Hey, you," he said softly.

"Hey, back. How is your first week out of the sling going?" she asked.

Mac gave her a moment to settle into her futon. "Okay. Really sore. But no," he said quickly, "I didn't overdo it." In fact, the shower and painkillers and the fact his arm was elevated meant the throbbing was easing by the minute. "How was your day?"

She beamed. "I got a nibble. I drafted an email and sent it to a bunch of engineering firms and got an invitation to come in and make a pitch." She held up a hand with her fingers crossed. "It's not until Friday, though."

"That's terrific."

"Since we're both on a roll, what do you say we talk about our next date? The St. Paul Saints are at home this weekend. Hot dogs, mini donuts, the sound of the bat hitting the ball." Lori lowered her voice. "Come on, you know you want to."

"I could get a room at a hotel that has a pool. We could have a pool party too."

"Finally! I haven't been swimming yet this year. Can you come?"

"Let me know what time to pick you up."

It was ridiculous. Even the idea of having a date with Lori made him feel better. He was still waiting for the other shoe to drop. He'd seen the worst of her when she worked for the Parkmans. He'd seen the best of her when she worked for him. This was the first time he'd see her on her home turf. Where would the middle ground lie?

It was also the first time she'd seen him in the same light. While her first impression hadn't been terrific, neither had his response. Now they were operating without the safety net of knowing she was leaving. If they wanted to see if they could go the distance, this date was their first step.

Anticipation got him through the rest of the week. His shoulder hurt every single day, but it was getting stronger. Resting it for the weekend would be the best thing he could do for it. The only stretching Mac planned to do was to give his girl a hug.

The first Saturday of June dawned bright and clear. Mac and Doug met at the marina at six-thirty. Mac got two hours of fishing in and was home, showered, and on the road by noon. He was mostly familiar with the Minnesota Twins' farm team, so he used the drive to listen to some podcasts so Lori's enthusiasm wouldn't leave him in the dust.

Before he knew it, he was pulling up to her place. Lori was waiting out front in a T-shirt and shorts, her black hair in a ponytail pulled through the back of a ball cap. She looked just like summer.

Lori bounded over to his truck and jumped into the cab as soon as he put it in park. She leaned over and kissed him, then broke into huge smile. "I missed you!"

"You, too."

"Come on. You introduced me to all the nooks and crannies of Holiday Beach. Let me show you around my town."

CHAPTER 25

LORI WAS ready to relax after the week she had. Baseball and sunshine were the perfect prescription.

It hadn't started badly. On Monday, she'd sent out yet another round of emails, applications, and résumé submissions. It was soul-sucking work. But at the end of the day, she'd received her first positive response. It wasn't for a job interview, but she'd finally made it to second base.

Then on Wednesday, Emily had arrived. She had two suitcases for her two-night stay, one of which was all hair and makeup products and a steamer for her clothes.

"I know they are going to have a wardrobe for me, but I want to arrive looking good," Emily said. "This is going to be a national commercial. If they like me…"

"The sky's the limit," Lori finished. Her stomach was in knots for her best friend. They had a simple meal for supper with no coffee, blueberries, or spinach. Lori helped Emily plan her route to the studio for the next day, and they crashed early.

Emily was awake before dawn on Wednesday. "This is it!"

"Break a leg!"

Since Lori didn't know when her friend would return home, she used the day to do some research for her "other" job. While *Modern Minnesota* turned down her article idea for communities going green, she wasn't ready to abandon it.

After two hours of significant internet research, she'd identified three other places to pitch the idea. Lori discovered she liked the work. She found some great green initiatives in Rochester and groups that encouraged recycling in schools. The more she found, the deeper she dug, until she had over two pages of ideas to work on.

Emily returned to her place at four o'clock.

"This seems early. Did everything go okay?" Lori asked.

Her friend's hair still had its natural curls, although it was styled differently than it had been when she'd left that morning. Emily pulled bobby pins out of her hair as she made herself comfortable on the futon. "It went fine. Good even, I think." She dropped a pile of pins onto the coffee table and gave her scalp a good rub. "They seemed happy. Now we wait."

Lori waited. "That's it?"

"I don't want to destroy the mystery of television by giving away all the "behind the scenes" secrets."

"That's not fair. Give me something!"

"I had a hair person, a makeup person, and a wardrobe person. It was like being a movie star," Emily gushed. "It was fabulous and I'm dying to do it again as soon as possible."

"That's better," Lori said. "Now let's celebrate."

Cupcakes and ice cream weren't for everybody, but

they were perfect for watching the *Santa Monica, E.R.* highlight special Lori found online.

Emily left first thing on Thursday morning, which gave Lori just enough time to clean up before Mac got there the next day. Her timing was great.

Because her grandma paid her an unexpected visit.

"Lori, how goes the employment search?" Arlene never beat around the bush.

"Good," she said honestly. Ever since she'd returned from Holiday Beach, her revitalize job hunt had begun to pay off. "I have an interview tomorrow morning. I also have two more articles due to online publications in the next two weeks."

"Paid articles, I assume. Not for exposure."

"Grandma, we both know people die of exposure. They're paid." That was part of the Baker work ethic. Know your worth.

Her grandma's shoulders came down a fraction. "I'm pleased to hear it. I was concerned you were sitting on your laurels while you entertained your friends. Who is the interview with?"

"Cartwright Engineering."

"Engineering? Why aren't you applying to architecture firms?"

"I'm doing that too. Engineers make buildings. Architects make them pretty. I'm speaking to them about consulting on their project to make their fixes and requirements more palatable to their clients."

Lori was surprised to receive a nod of approval for her unconventional idea. "That's a novel approach. If it doesn't pan out, let me know. I suppose I could ask around at the club to see if anyone has any leads for you, but I'd rather do that if you have another job on the table so you don't look desperate."

"Thanks, Grandma. I'll let you know how the interview goes." The timing wasn't going to get any better. "I'm going out tomorrow with Mac again. He's coming in for a baseball game."

"He's not planning on staying here, is he?"

Having a female friend stay over was one thing. Her grandma would never approve of a male guest. As she loved to say, it was her house, her rules. Until Lori was back in her own place, she had to live by them. "He's staying at the Longfellow Park in St. Paul." She'd been surprised by the choice since it was a high-end hotel, but Mac said Roy got him a family discount. "They have a pool, so I'm meeting him there tomorrow for a swim before he checks out."

"The Longfellow Park?" The golden-haired woman sniffed, then left without a goodbye.

"This meeting had better pay off," Lori muttered to herself.

It wasn't a no. It wasn't a yes either. Her interviewers were a senior engineer at the firm and their marketing-slash-customer service manager. They'd talked with her for over an hour about what services she could provide and how it would benefit the company and their clients. Lori had left with a promise that they'd liked her proposal and would get back to her, with the understanding she wasn't going to be getting a job offer anytime soon.

Win some, lose some. It wasn't a terrible way to end the week.

Saturday morning dawned bright and clear. She was ready and waiting for Mac after he texted he was at a gas station ten minutes from her house.

"We're a little early. Should we have a snack before we get to the ballpark?" he asked.

Of all the things she loved about Holiday Beach, there was one gaping hole in her heart that it couldn't fill. There were no fast-food restaurants in town. Every now and then, a girl just needed greasy fries and a milkshake.

The Saints didn't play on the same field as the Twins. Their home field held about seven thousand people. They were playing a favorite rival, so the place was filled by the time she and Mac finished touring the concourse and found their seats. She got a bucket of mini donuts to share. Mac bought two bottles of water to keep them hydrated while they sat in the evening sun.

It was a perfect night for a ball game. The day's heat lingered a little as the sun went down. Lori had expected that and brought a light jacket, but she didn't expect to need it. A light breeze blew across the field, chasing away the few mosquitoes buzzing around the stands looking for a free meal.

The announcers asked them to stand for the national anthem, then read the player rosters for both teams. Just before the ump yelled "Play ball!" he reminded fans it was fireworks night and they should stay after the game for a display.

"How romantic," Lori said.

"How's that?"

"You and me alone under the stars and with fireworks going off overhead."

"Alone with all the other people here watching the game."

She leaned over and whispered in his ear. "If you're thinking about all these other people when you're kissing me, you're doing it wrong."

Then she helpfully held his drink as he choked on his donut.

Unfortunately, the game was a blowout for the opposing team. The Saints kept it from being a no-hitter with a lucky in-field home run with the help of two unforced errors at the bottom of the seventh. A lot of fans had left early in disappointment when the lead stretched to double digits, but Lori was determined to wait it out.

The wind died, leaving the day's heat infiltrating from the city surrounding them. "Are you ready for the show?" she asked.

Mac wrapped his arm around her shoulders and pulled her closer. "I always enjoy a good fireworks display. I'd like to remind you, though, we have award-winning fireworks in Holiday Beach for Independence Day, and you haven't said a word about your plans yet."

She thought he was teasing, but one look into his eyes convinced her he was serious. "I already told you I was coming!"

"But when? Thursday? Friday? Are you staying with Emily or Gloria? Or somebody else? Are you going to let me take you fishing? You—"

Before Mac could continue, a boom echoed across the dark ball field. A streak of light shot into the sky and exploded into a white starburst with a crack that filled the night. It was followed by a crimson one and then a blue one. The booms and pops and cracks were the only soundtrack to the light show, but they were enough. Especially when they were punctuated by the oohs and aahs of the crowd.

"You're missing it," Lori whispered in Mac's ear as he strained his neck to see a particularly high display.

"Missing what?"

"Your chance to kiss me."

He tore his gaze from the sky and looked deep into her eyes, then smiled slowly. "Let's make our own fireworks."

The noise and light faded away when their lips touched. "You know, Mac, it wouldn't take much to fall in love with you," she whispered. They'd had a rocky start, but she had no doubts about him now.

"Wouldn't take much? Catch up, would you? I'm already in love with you," he whispered back.

What could she say about the rest of the dazzling display overhead? Not much, because the man could really kiss.

CHAPTER 26

His current company was underdressed and not nearly attractive as other people he'd spent time with lately. They were sweaty, dirty, and going through his beer at a rapid rate.

"I'll bet you wish I was Lori," Josh said as he attempted to flick a bottle cap into the trash can and missed.

"You have no idea," Mac replied.

He was supposed to be spending a relaxing Saturday afternoon with his girlfriend. They'd planned for her to drive to Holiday Beach late Friday afternoon. They'd have a walk on the boardwalk along the beach, and she'd crash on Emily's sofa for the night. On Saturday morning, they were supposed to go fishing. Mac had already bought a new cooler with cupholders in the lid to hold their coffees while they reeled in their catches.

He had plans. Romantic plans after their night under the fireworks. But one call on Thursday afternoon had blown them all up like a double-powered firecracker.

"I have good news and bad news times two," Lori had said in her unexpected lunchtime video call.

"What's the good news?"

"I have a job interview for an architect position at an established firm with a good reputation. And I am doing an interview for a paid website article with a local composting expert."

He'd been thrilled for her. She was a machine when it came to sending out applications and queries and contacting friends and former coworkers for leads. He wanted her hard work to pay off. "That sounds great. What's the bad news?"

"The architecture firm is in Chicago. The job interview is a Zoom call on Saturday afternoon."

"Oh."

"Yeah, oh," Lori had said, matching his flat tone. "It's in the middle of the afternoon, not even in the morning."

At first, he'd thought she could still come to Holiday Beach. She'd get there too late in the evening to do anything on Saturday night, but they could have a few hours on Sunday. That was better than nothing. Then she dropped a second bomb.

"And the composting interview is on Sunday morning. It was the only time he had free," Lori had continued.

"If that's when you've got to do it."

She took a deep breath, and he was afraid of yet another round of bad news. It was anything but. "It really sucks when two people who love each other can't see each other."

"It does. But when two people love each other, they'll wait. Right?" he asked, wanting to make sure he'd heard what he heard.

"Right."

Despite that burst of joy, the rest of their chat was an incredibly depressing conversation where he tried to be supportive of her interviews. They decided to postpone her visit for a week.

With the lack of a fishing partner for Saturday morning, he'd called Josh to fulfill a promise to take him out on the lake. He was a poor substitute, but an excellent fishing buddy. "I can't believe the luck we had this morning," Josh said.

"It was pretty good," Mac admitted.

"It was definitely worth the day we spent installing all that drywall. Speaking of walls, they look great. I can't believe you're almost done." Josh looked around the room admiringly.

He was. Everything from the ceilings to the floor and the light fixtures to the baseboards was finished in the living room and dining room. He'd installed the kitchen cupboards the previous week and was now only waiting for the countertops and backsplash. The downstairs bedroom was only waiting on closet doors. It was the final details that seemed to take forever. "I'm so close," Mac agreed. "But I have one big project left down here." He tilted his head to the still open staircase.

Josh laughed loudly. "Why do I have the feeling I'm about to be offered another morning in your boat if I volunteer to help with your slat-wall project?"

"Because you're an incredibly smart, talented independent business owner like myself who can spot an opportunity when he sees one. Not to mention, you're nearly as good-looking as me too," Mac said. He batted his eyes at his friend for added effect.

"Yeah, yeah. I'll help in exchange for another day in your boat," Josh agreed. "Summer is slow at the gym, anyway. We get a few out-of-towners who want day passes, but most people are on vacation or getting their workouts by working in the yard."

"I don't have plans because Lori had to cancel. Am I interrupting anything on your schedule?" Mac didn't want to inconvenience his friend.

"No. Unfortunately. My last couple of dates with Sandra from Bixby fizzled due to an extreme lack of chemistry." Josh pulled on the work gloves Mac handed him and walked to the pile of cut and sanded lumber in the middle of the living room.

"I thought you liked her."

"It all worked on paper. The dating app said we were a good match. But there was no spark. I guess I'm back to Hopeless in Holiday Beach," Josh said.

Mac knew the comment was only half in jest. Dating in a small town was rough. The population was small enough that it was easy to end up dating somebody else's ex, which made for awkward meetings all over town. "You'll always have your fishing rod."

"That might be part of the problem. But not today. Let's get your staircase finished."

The nail gun was hard on his shoulder, but with Josh's help, they quickly got the boards in place and secured. Soon they were admiring it from their lawn chairs as they celebrated another job well done.

"Speaking of Lori—" Mac started.

"We weren't," Josh interrupted, laughing, "but go ahead."

"I was wondering if you'd heard anything about any small office spaces available for rent in the Holiday Beach Business Center. I figure as the president of the Chamber of Commerce, you'd know if any leases had been signed lately."

That was the idea Mac had been working on for the last couple of weeks in between his regular job and construction on his house. There was no way Lori could open her own architecture firm, not in Holiday Beach. But a small, one-person office? That was a lot less overhead. Between the good work she'd done with them and Helen Pham's word-of-mouth after the design success of her daughter's geometric walls, Lori had a new reputation in town. Whether it was a viable business was a conversation he needed to have with her in person.

"I know of some offices that are available," Josh said.

"Take a look and see if any of the smaller ones are still up for grabs, would you?"

"No problem."

Mac handed Josh another beer. "You aren't just a pretty face." All he had to do now was have the information in hand when he broached the topic in person with Lori in a week. He hoped she was as excited as him at the idea. It'd be perfect.

CHAPTER 27

HER LIFE HAD TURNED UPSIDE DOWN in the last week.
It had gone from mostly a mess to totally bonkers. Lori
desperately needed a breather, but she didn't have time.
All she could spare was an hour.

Fortunately, she had someone to spend it with. Lori
texted Doug to find out where the brothers were working,
then timed her arrival to get her there a little before noon
with a takeout lunch for two in the passenger seat
beside her.

The June sun beat down on the yards and gardens of
the street. Her own Mackenzie Brothers Painting hat did
nothing to protect her from the glare. But it was much
better than the heat of the city that never seemed to dissi-
pate, even after the sun went down. Summer had arrived
in Holiday Beach in earnest, and she was there for it. The
drive from the city had been a treat—windows down,
music on the radio, a cold drink in the console. Lori could
get used to a summer softened by a breeze off the lake.

Mac stood outside when she pulled to the curb. She
grinned as he did a double take at her car and then broke

into a jog, heading in her direction. "What are you doing here?" he asked as she stepped up to give him a hug.

"Surprise!"

"I'll say." He pulled her close and gave her a kiss, smelling of sweat and sunshine and paint. "But I'll ask again, what are you doing here?"

"It's a long story. Can I tell you over lunch? I brought drinks and sandwiches for two." It was a saga that needed an explanation.

They sat on the tailgate of Mac's truck. Lori handed out their meals, and Mac kept smiling at her. "I can't believe you're here. For how long?"

"Lunch only. It's part of my wacky tale." She cracked the bottle of lemonade and took a drink to wet her throat. "Okay. Here we go. On Saturday, I interviewed with the architecture firm in Chicago. They weren't actually hiring. I discovered when I got there it was a courtesy interview my grandmother arranged with a friend at her bridge club. There was never a job at their office."

"Oh, that sucks! And it ruined our weekend plans."

"Yeah. But after the interview, I got a call from Cartwright Engineering. They're the company I interviewed with a couple of weeks ago. They asked if I wanted to do an independent consultation for them out near Thief River Falls. The firm they usually used from the Minneapolis-St. Paul metro area said it wasn't worth their associates' time to make the trip to the north end of the state."

"I can't blame them. That's in the back of beyond," Mac said. He wasn't kidding. That was at least another two hours north of Holiday Beach. "Are they paying you?"

"Some. It's a onetime contract to test the idea out. I'm

getting a small consultant fee, and they're springing for mileage. It'll basically cover my gas and my meals. But it's a start, right?"

"Right!"

She had to turn an ugly, retrofitted commercial property into a sleek lobby to a business center, taking into account all the structural requirements that seemed to center in the main entrance. It was going to be a challenge. But it was architecture she was being paid for. "This is a feel-each-other-out job. Obviously, I won't be able to live on what they're paying, but for now I'll do the work. I'll have to figure out how to turn it into a full-time thing if it works. But for now, a job and lunch with my man. Win-win!"

"I still can't believe you're here. Will I see you on the way home too?"

"I think I can arrange that with my boss. Who is me. I've got to tell you, Mac. Being self-employed has its advantages."

"It does. You can choose your own hours, so long as it works with your clients. On the other hand, sometimes the boss is completely unreasonable and makes you work weekends and holidays."

"And cancel dates with your boyfriend. I filed a complaint about that one. It went nowhere," Lori joked. But aside from that, running her own business had never been something she'd considered. She'd always worked for somebody else. She did her work and got a paycheck at the end of the week. Being responsible for everything was stressful, but also exciting. It was an intriguing possibility if she could afford it.

"How did the compost interview go?"

"I now have more knowledge about worms and vermicomposting than I'll ever need in this lifetime." They both got a laugh out of that. "But I also have two hundred dollars in the bank. That's car insurance for the month." One success at a time.

"I approve of any job that allows for surprise lunches."

Their impromptu date ended much too soon. "I have to be in Thief River Falls by two o'clock for the walk-through. But I can visit for a little while on my way back," she said.

Mac walked her to her car. "This was amazing. Unexpected, but fantastic. How is your schedule looking for this weekend?" he asked.

"Right now, good. But if I get another consulting job..." She'd want to take it. She couldn't afford to turn down work. Lori hoped he understood.

From the look on his face, he did, although it was disappointing. "I get it. I've been there. When we were just getting started, Doug and I had to sacrifice a lot of weekends. But you still have some regular nine-to-five applications out there. Those could still turn into opportunities," Mac said hopefully.

"It would be nice," she agreed. But this was good too. It was too bad she couldn't have both.

CHAPTER 28

He was done. The main floor was completely constructed and decorated, down to the last pin nail and inch of grout, and it looked fantastic. Mac looked around his house and didn't try to hide the pride coursing through him. He'd done it. Finally.

Blood, sweat, and tears had turned a rough patch of scrub brush-filled land into a home. One he could comfortably live in. Once he finished the upstairs, it would be a two-story, four-bedroom, three-bath house, with an open kitchen, living room and dining room on the main floor and an extended deck off the back. It was fifteen minutes by car and thirty by bike to his office. The marina was even closer. It had everything he'd ever wanted.

There was only one problem with it, and it was the same thing Doug had pointed out. It was an awfully big place for only one person.

At least that wouldn't be a problem for this evening. Lori was coming over for dinner. She was his first official guest, and he was doing it up like the very special occasion it was. The steaks were ready for the barbecue, the salad was chilling in the crisper, and the baked potatoes were already in a slow cooker on the counter. The table on the deck was covered in a borrowed tablecloth and had a heavy vase filled with wildflowers to hold it down.

A knock on the door told him Lori was right on time.

She gasped when he opened the door. "Show me everything," she demanded.

Lori toured the living room and gushed over the stone heat shield behind the woodstove that had been installed after the afternoon she'd spent helping with the drywall and plaster. She hugged the kitchen cabinets and counter-tops and pronounced them to be perfection.

But when she saw the staircase, she fell silent. She knew he'd used her suggestion of a slat wall, but seeing it in all its glory was enough to strike anyone dumb. At least he thought so. "Okay," Lori eventually said. "I'm a genius."

That broke the spell. "It was a good idea. I'll give you twelve percent of the credit for it looking so good."

She looked at him for the first time since he'd opened the door. "Hi, there."

"Hi, back." Mac had seen her four days earlier on her way back to Minneapolis. On that trip, she'd brought a black coffee to the house, but she hadn't made it inside. Instead, she told him his deck would be perfect for Tai Chi if he wanted to start, but she had to get back on the road twenty minutes later if she wanted to get back to the city by midnight. She texted that she was working on the project all day Tuesday, Wednesday, and Thursday and had turned it in at noon on Friday. Then she'd jumped in her car to come out to Holiday Beach. "Now that you've had the tour, can I say hello properly?"

He really enjoyed having both his arms back so he could hold her while he kissed her. She fit against him perfectly.

"Yes, hello. Feel free to say it as often as you want." Then she jerked back. "Wait! I have an official house-warming gift for you."

Lori left him standing in the middle of the living room while she raced back to her car. She returned with a gift bag in one hand and a potted plant in the other. "Happy 'Your house is move-in ready although you've already been living in it' Day! These are for you. They go together."

The plant had fat, almost round branches and no leaves. There were small spikes along the edges. He gently squeezed it, and it squished between his fingers like it was full of water. "It's an aloe plant," she told him. "You can cut a piece off and rub the sap on a burn. I figured you might have a few accidents while you're getting used to the new woodstove."

"Thanks. That's a great idea." He could picture the plant getting a lot of use. "What's in the bag?"

"Open it and see."

He laughed. Loudly. Lori's grin matched his own as he pulled black, elbow-high oven mitts from the bag. "These will help too."

"I don't want you to injure yourself again. I almost got you a lightning rod, but I couldn't find one I liked."

"These are awesome."

Dinner was peaceful. The early evening sun hit the treetops, throwing shade across the deck. It kept the still air from being too hot. Birds in the trees tweeted a constant melody, interrupted by the occasional solo from a chittering squirrel. They caught up on all the Holiday

Beach news. Lori surprised him with a couple of additions she'd heard from the girls' network.

"How did your assignment in Thief River Falls go?" Mac asked.

She froze. "It was interesting," she finally said.

"Do you want to talk about it?"

Lori hesitated again. "It's a complicated situation that will take some time. Are you sure you want to get into it? We could just enjoy tonight."

Then he understood what she was saying. Dating was easy. Fun times, some good night kisses. It was easy to fall in love. Deep conversations were a big step to a new relationship level. "I think a big conversation needs couch cushions and not patio furniture," he said.

"Okay."

She sat beside him at the beginning. "The job itself went really well. I understood the engineer's requirements. The client was a dream. They knew exactly what they wanted and listened when I told them what they could and couldn't do. Honestly, I don't think that part could have gone better."

"That sounds promising," Mac said encouragingly.

"Exactly! I may not have another one that good again."

"Is that a problem?"

"Yes. No, not really." She squeezed his hand, then stood to pace in front of the sofa. "Here's the thing. Cartwright Engineering is reviewing my report and will be talking to the client later next week. They said that if they're happy with it, they'll talk to me about being a permanent consultant."

"That's great." Especially if it meant she could detour to Holiday Beach when she was in the area."

"But I can't survive on what they're paying. Not if I have to commute from Minneapolis for every job. Like I said, I barely broke even on the last job. Besides, I don't think that one company could have enough assignments to give me full-time hours."

"Could you get work for more than one company?"

"That's the thing. I think so."

Lori collapsed beside him and nudged him until he put his arm around her. He complied. "What if... I can't believe I'm even thinking this. What if I started my own consulting company? What if I specialized in rural properties? If I get an agreement in place with Cartwright Engineering, I know I could get on with another one. There might be enough business here for me. But how do I start? Bakers are behind-the-scenes people. We're the power behind the throne. We don't start businesses. If they fail, we'll be laughing stocks. Although I won't have to worry about starving to death. If I failed publicly, my grandma would kill me."

He waited. "Did you breathe during any of that?"

"Who can breathe when their life is upside down?" She sighed. "I don't know what I was thinking. I got so excited about one job that I turned it into my own personal empire."

"Do you want to vent to me, or do you want to brainstorm some options?" He wanted it to be the second. A million ideas cascaded in his head, like how she could set up her own business, which computer programs she needed to run projections to see if her idea was viable, and places in Holiday Beach she could use for her office. But it would be a lot of work. A tidal wave of things to do.

As much as he liked Lori, he still didn't know her that well. He didn't know if she'd want the responsibility, let alone if she could handle it. But he had a feeling she could. He thought she'd be great at it.

Or he could pat her on the back and tell her to keep applying to places where she could be an excellent employee who didn't have to worry about running a business on top of being an architect.

All he had to know was which side she was going to land on.

CHAPTER 29

ONCE SHE STARTED TALKING to Mac, she couldn't stop. Lori didn't know what was going to come out of her mouth next, but every idea, every hope, and every fear spilled all over his living room.

The more she talked about opening her own architecture firm, the more she wanted it. She knew it wouldn't be what she'd dreamed of when she showed up in class on her first day of college. Designing mega-mansions for billionaire clients was a nice fantasy, but she'd discovered she also found satisfaction in smaller projects. The gratitude she received from giving people the houses of their dreams was incredibly satisfying. She could continue to design castles in the sky; the ones on the ground would be more than enough to pay her bills.

Even better, she was good at it. She turned problems into works of beauty.

But there were a million steps between having the desire to open her own firm and actually doing it. The first was to decide if she even wanted to try. Her grandma would not approve. But she couldn't live her life that way.

Lori took a deep breath.

"Brainstorm," she said.

She'd said it aloud. There was no going back now.

"First of all, I think you should make Holiday Beach your home base and open your office here," Mac said. He was grinning wildly, but she could tell he was serious.

"Why?"

"Because it will be much easier for us to have date nights," he replied instantly. "But also, it's central to a huge area." Mac looked around his apartment and shook his head in disappointment. "This isn't the place to have this conversation."

"It isn't?"

"Not at all." He stood. "Come on. I want to show you something."

Her decision was causing new results to explode like a string of lit firecrackers. "Right now?"

Mac pulled her to her feet. "No time like the present."

She let him drive and didn't say a word until he pulled into a parking spot in front of the Holiday Beach Business Center. "You take me to the nicest places. I know we're new, but do I have to explain how date night works?"

"Have faith, Lori."

"I'm trying!"

Mac unlocked the building's front doors with his own key, then locked it behind them. Lori had never been in the building before. It had been a school at one point; the design was still evident in the floor plan. But the town had transitioned it into an office complex. Each of the old classrooms had been turned into an independent workspace.

Some companies had converted two or three rooms into large offices. Others were contained in a single room. But each had a sign on the door, marking it clearly. Mac showed her around the building: there was a realty office, a computer-repair center, a website designer, a photographer, and a four-seasons maintenance company. He stopped walking in front of an unmarked door.

"What's this one?"

"It used to be a printing company, but it went out of business a couple of months ago. We repainted it just before you came to town. But it could be the new home of Baker Architecture, or whatever you decide to name your new company." He pulled another keychain from his pocket. "Do you want to look around?"

"Why do you have the key?"

"I asked Josh for it."

"Why?"

He shrugged. "Wishful thinking after you surprised me at lunch. I wanted to see if it would work as an office for you. What do you think?"

The office was small, about half the size of his at Mackenzie Brothers Painting's headquarters. She could set her drafting table in one corner, and it could double as a desk. She'd have just enough room for a credenza and filing cabinet on the other wall and a client table in the middle of the room.

But she didn't need more than that. The small office was more than enough room for one person. "When is it available?"

"Immediately." Then he told her the price. It wasn't cheap, but it was only a fraction of what she'd pay for the same space in the city.

"I need a calculator. Tomorrow," she amended. "I've

derailed our date enough for one evening." Her head spun with possibilities.

"I helped. It wasn't a normal date, but I think it's our most memorable one yet," Mac said.

"You're not kidding. Until tomorrow, at least. I have a plan."

"I thought it was my turn to plan our date."

"It should be, but I'm hoping you'll let me pick. I heard of something I'd love to try with you. Besides, you took me on a field trip tonight," she wheedled. "It was practically a roller coaster. What I have in mind isn't nearly as mind-bending."

"Fine, you can pick our date tomorrow. But I'm buying ice cream afterward."

"We'll discuss it," Lori hedged. "But first, let's go back to your place. You can tell me any other wishful thinking you've been doing about me moving back to Holiday Beach." She'd imagined Mac might have considered getting her to return to Holiday Beach, but she'd never guessed he would have done prep work to support his arguments. Perhaps he knew her better than she thought.

CHAPTER 30

IT WAS HER IDEA. That's what Mac would say to anyone who gave him a dirty look for taking his girlfriend fishing at six o'clock on a Saturday morning. Lori had insisted on the full fishing experience. In return, he promised to introduce her to the world of crepes the Atlas Restaurant had as their Sunday morning breakfast special, although they'd do that at a more reasonable hour.

So here he was at ten to six in the morning, parked outside Emily's apartment building. Lori appeared in shorts and a T-shirt under her windbreaker. She had a small nylon bag instead of a purse and a huge but sleepy smile.

"I'll buy the coffee if you buy the worms," she said after she kissed him hello.

"I'll buy both," Mac said. "From different places."

"Can you buy worms and coffee at the same place?" Lori asked in concern.

"Yes, from the Pollux Maritime Gas Station. I wouldn't recommend it."

"The coffee or the worms?"

"The coffee. We'll stop at By the Cup."

They broke in his new cooler in style. The cupholders kept their coffees from spilling as he steered them to his favorite cove. The water was so smooth they didn't spill a single drop.

The forecast predicted the day ahead as a scorcher, and they felt that as soon as the sun rose fully over the horizon. The reflection off the glasslike surface made them both reach for their sunglasses. Bird calls echoed across the water, and the nearest boat was several hundred feet away on another inlet.

"I can see this being relaxing," Lori admitted.

"Do you want to cast a line?" Mac offered. "The fishing is actually optional."

"Oh, no, I want the whole Mackenzie fishing experience. I'll even bait my own hook." She wore a fiercely determined look, but there was fear in her eyes at the thought of handling worms.

He took pity on her. "Baiting a hook is lesson three, so I'll do it for you today."

Her shoulders dropped. "Awesome."

Mac did his best to direct her on how to cast. She did it perfectly on her third try. So perfectly her bobber disappeared in less than a minute.

"What do I do?" she gasped.

"Reel it in!" It took some teamwork and a fumbled net, but eventually they pulled her catch into the boat. "What a beauty!" It wasn't the biggest trout Mac had ever seen, but it would make an excellent meal for two. "You just caught dinner."

Lori beamed with pride as he took a picture of her holding her catch.

An hour later, they returned to his slip. "It's a good

thing you had some luck this morning. Otherwise we'd be coming in empty-handed," Mac said as he helped her out of the boat. He'd caught a few perches, but they were too small to keep. "What do you think of the full Mackenzie fishing experience?" he asked.

"It was fun. I don't think it's something I'd want to do every weekend morning, but it would be fun to do every once in a while," Lori said.

It was an answer he could live with. Taking Lori out to share a morning on the lake on occasion and going out with a buddy for some serious fishing on the other days. It gave him the best of both worlds. "That sounds perfect."

She grabbed his arm as they stepped off the dock. "Is she waving at us?" She pointed to a tall blonde woman standing next to a white van at the gas pump.

Julie Handler waved again, then motioned for them to join her. Mac threw the cooler and fish bucket into the back of his truck, then took Lori's hand and led her across the street. Julie was still cool towards her, but at least the outright animosity had faded in the last couple of months.

"Guess who sold all the tin ceiling tiles she had in stock to the contractor doing the kitchen ceiling at the Holiday House?" she asked.

"That's fantastic!" Lori exclaimed. "I am so glad you were able to get rid of them."

"Mac said it was your idea. I wanted to say thanks." Julie offered them a tentative smile, which Lori returned wholeheartedly. She'd worked hard to overcome her reputation around town, and Julie had been one of the last holdouts. Of course, Julie had also borne the brunt of Lori's disastrous Parkman demands. With this latest news, she might be over the hump when it came to her past.

"Those are going to look so good," Lori said.

"If I get photos, I'll pass them on to Mac to show you."

"I'd appreciate that."

"Thanks for letting us know," he said.

"I'm not done," Julie said. "I have all the gossip this morning. I went by your house to give you the good news. You weren't there, but I saw something very interesting involving your neighbors."

He groaned. "How much damage did they do? Is my house still standing?" He wished he were joking.

"Your property is absolutely fine. There's a new addition at the end of the driveway next door, though."

"Did the Parkmans finally name their house?" Lori asked.

"They did! It's called "For Sale" according to the sign that just went up." Julie grinned as she delivered her news.

"You're kidding!"

"I'm not. All construction has stopped, and they have put the whole unfinished property on the market," Julie elaborated. "I got that directly from the real estate agent. What I've heard unofficially is that no contractor within a hundred miles is willing to work with them anymore. There's something about a pool, but nobody local knows anything about that."

Lori snorted, drawing attention from them both. "Obviously, I can't say anything about my former clients, but in general, what do you think the cost would be to have an in-ground pool installed?"

Mac laughed. "Are you kidding? With all the bedrock around here? That price tag has to be pushing six figures."

Lori gasped. "I figured mid-five."

Julie shook her head. "Mac's closer. The Dempseys

looked into it a few years ago. I wonder how much the Parkmans sank into that property. And what they're asking for it."

"I don't care. All I want are nice, quiet neighbors."

"Better luck next time. Who knows, you might get lucky," Julie said. "Anyway, I'm off to spread the news. See you around."

Lori was quiet when they climbed into the truck cab. "I'm dying to know the details. I know I said I washed my hands of the Parkmans, but that's some really good dirt. Why are they selling? Who's going to buy it? What happened with the other contractors? I need to know, Mac!"

"I'll do some snooping for you." And for himself. He wished he was sympathetic to his neighbors' plight, but they'd dug themselves into such a big hole in the community, they never would have climbed out of it. Lori had barely been able to, and she'd just been one soldier in their construction army. Nobody would miss them if they moved on to greener pastures. "I guess that means Kurt Crabb won't be coming back for a follow-up on their place."

"Guess not."

He couldn't get over the good news. "Let's go get your fish on ice and then head into town to celebrate this news. It's been a fantastic morning. I don't know how it could get any better."

CHAPTER 31

LORI THOUGHT he'd jinxed it. Her luck hadn't been terrific over the last few months. She'd have one good thing pop up among a field of bad luck. But Mac was insistent on celebrating. She didn't blame him. If the Parkmans had been her neighbors, she would have thrown a good riddance party for them if she learned they were leaving.

But the day wasn't finished with her.

"Did you get all the pictures you needed of cottages in the area for your article?" Mac asked after their lunch of barbecued hot dogs.

"Yes. There was a gorgeous A-frame on the other side of the lake. I spoke to the owners, and they let me take some close-ups." The blog post was scheduled for next week, and she was getting full credit.

"Did you check out any of the cabins on Moony Creek, around the bend from where it empties into Star Lake?"

"No. Moony Creek? And Star Lake?"

"It's a coincidence. Honestly. Moony Creek is named

after the miner who discovered it during the Holiday Mine copper boom. There are four cottages up there. The families who bought the land were from Switzerland or Austria or somewhere very Bavarian. They look odd compared to the others around the lake, but the four of them, in context with the woods, look like a scene out of some alpine European documentary out of the 1950s. Do you want to go see?"

"Sure." They headed up the highway, but they'd only driven a couple of miles past the marina when Lori yelled. "Stop! Pull over!"

Mac cranked the wheel and skidded to a stop on the shoulder. "What?"

She couldn't form the words. All she could do was point at a billboard on the far side of the ditch. Mac stared at it for a moment, blinked, and then looked at it again.

"It's a sign."

"I can see that."

"No. A *sign* sign. For you," Mac insisted.

She wished she could argue. But she couldn't. Because that was exactly what she thought. "Let's go look at those cottages. Maybe I can take some pictures. But then I need you to drive me home."

Neither of them moved. The beautiful billboard in front of them was too mesmerizing. It was a simple rectangle. White background. Dark-blue type. "New cottage development approved. Twenty lots for sale. Build the cottage of your dreams." And a name and phone number for the real estate office in the business center.

Lori was here. On the ground. An architect who'd designed cottages. Ready to go. With knowledge of the area and of local contractors. The opportunity couldn't be more obvious if a beam of sunlight had split the clouds and shone directly onto the sign with a rainbow leading the way.

They were pulling into Mac's driveway before she realized it. "What about the cottages?"

"Darling Lori, you are in no shape to look at cottages. There are stars in your eyes, and you're talking to yourself. Do you want to know what you're saying?"

"I hope it's something like "Do it!" and not "Run away!" because..." She gulped. "Because I think I'm ready to do this. Mac, can I do this?"

Her grandma always called the Bakers the powers behind the curtain. But Lori didn't want to hide anymore. She was a good architect. Despite the Parkmans, other people had thought so. She was getting nowhere trying to do things the Baker way, looking for other people to help her. Maybe it was time to help herself.

As soon as her grandma caught wind of her plan, the generous offer of a rent-free place to stay would be rescinded. Lori didn't like it, but fair was fair. Grandma's house, grandma's rules. Bakers did not take chances, especially ones that could lead to public failure.

On the other hand, in the family's well-discussed history, the Bakers had never left a mark in the world either. No works of art, no streets named after them. People don't remember folks who didn't risk it all.

"Don't answer that. I can do this," she said before he could answer. "Do I want to do this?" She needed to do a deep dive into her finances and figure out what it would cost to get her business up and running. She needed a place to live and a place to work. She needed clients. A lot of them. Fortunately, she had an outrageous nest egg. It was supposed to be a down payment for her first house.

What if she used it to buy what she needed for her first business?

"I'm here for whatever you decide. You have my support. All of it."

"I'm going to be emotionally needy and physically absent if I do this."

"I can be emotionally present. And how absent could you be if you're working in Holiday Beach? Five minutes with you is worth five hours with anybody else."

Lori stared deeply into Mac's honey-brown eyes. He meant every word.

"You know, I'm considering walking away from my whole previous life to move to a town where I have an idea and a boyfriend. It must be love."

"What do I have to do to turn this consideration into a commitment?" he asked.

"Don't let me quit."

Mac kissed her. "Never."

CHAPTER 32

SHE WAS DREAMING. She was in a castle, surrounded by towers and a massive stone wall. She was on a feather bed, but her body hurt after battling a dragon.

Lori opened her eyes. It was pitch black. She'd hung real curtains on the window, but there was no light coming through them anyway since the entire wall was blocked, floor to ceiling, with stacks of boxes.

Most of the tiny studio was boxes, and the few pieces of furniture she'd shoehorned into the room were also covered with boxes. That was what happened when a person downsized from a regular, one-bedroom apartment into a single kitchen-living room-bedroom floor plan. That explained the dream about the castle and towers.

The dragon was metaphorical. It had been a beast of a job moving everything from her grandma's garage back to Holiday Beach. The past few days had been a whirlwind. She and Mac had run numbers all Sunday. By the time Monday morning rolled around, she was committed. So committed, she let Mac contact Sarah Napier at the

Holiday Beach Business Center, and she'd signed her intent to lease before she returned to Minneapolis.

She had to let her grandma know what was going on. Arlene Baker was not impressed with her decision. Lori counted herself lucky that her grandma had allowed her to the end of week to empty her apartment above the garage. Luckily, she was already mostly packed. A couple of things didn't make the cut, but she'd been ruthless when she'd lost her old apartment. This time, she was finally ready to relegate the used cat tree to the trash. She had pictures of her Georgie. The rest was just stuff. It still took two days to pack.

Luckily, Lucy hadn't rented the studio she'd vacated the previous month, so she got that back. Even better, her lease at the Holiday Beach Business Center had been approved almost overnight. She suspected her references had something to do with it. She was committed to a year in each property, which meant she had twelve months to sink or swim.

Two round trips per day for two days, at three hours each way, meant she'd spent twenty-four hours behind the wheel over the past two days. Between that and the labor of packing everything, she was dead on her feet. When she fell asleep in her apartment for the first time on the first of July, she hadn't woken until midmorning on the second.

The rest of the second was moving furniture into the office. That had allowed her just enough space to turn around in her apartment. Which she was doing now. What she didn't understand was why she was awake at such an unreasonable. Her plan had been to sleep until eleven and then meet Mac for lunch at the Atlas Restaurant at a minute to noon before her afternoon kicked off. After a hectic week, she deserved to sleep in.

A muffled sound came from the hall. "Lori, are you awake in there?"

She felt her way through the dark room until she reached the door. "Mac?" she asked sleepily. She opened the door to see sunlight streaming through the window at the end of the hall. "Is it noon?"

"Not yet."

"You know I love you, but I'm going back to bed. I'm exhausted."

"You can't. There's been an accident at the Holiday Beach Business Center."

"That's too bad."

"That's your office, sleepyhead."

That was enough to wake her up. "What happened? What time is it?"

Mac reached through the open door and gently pushed her back into her apartment. "It's a little after eight. Get dressed and I'll drive you down there."

She found a pair of capri pants, a clean T-shirt, and a ball cap. Then she pulled her long black curls into a pony-tail, splashed some water on her face, and brushed her teeth. She was out the door in less than five minutes.

It didn't mean she was awake, though. "Where are we going again?"

"To your new office. Are you always like this when you get up?"

"Pretty much. Why are we going to my office at eight in the morning? I don't have any appointments." She would love to have an appointment waiting for her first thing in the morning. She'd love one at any time of day, but it was only the third of July, and she'd spent the second day of the month decorating the place with nary a client in sight. It would take more than twenty-four hours to get her business up and running.

Although, all she had left to do was find clients, design amazing buildings, and take the checks to the bank. That was just three things. No problem.

She was already prepared to start introducing herself to potential clients. Although she'd barely moved in, she was having her official office open house that afternoon, when the building was open to invite visitors to check out all the businesses Holiday Beach had to offer while they were in town for Independence Day weekend.

At least, that had been the plan.

"A water pipe burst. Your office is in the flood zone. Sorry, Trouble."

The walls Mac had painted a soft, barely-there mint green a couple of months earlier were now dripping water. Two ceiling panels lay on the soaked carpet, and half a dozen more were stained yellow. A puddle was slowly making its way to the door. But that wasn't the most shocking thing she saw. "Where's my stuff?" Lori demanded.

She didn't have much. She'd moved her kitchen table and chairs into the office to act as boardroom furniture, which did her the double favor of getting them out of her apartment where they wouldn't fit, anyway. But the two short filing cabinets that made up her credenza were also missing, along with her drafting table and stool. The only things left in the office were her coat rack and a stack of three tote bins in the corner.

"Yeah, we had to get rid of them," Mac said.

"You threw them out?"

"What? No! We had to move them to access the leak."

Mac rubbed her back as she tried to catch her breath after witnessing all her plans get washed away. "Here's the woman who's going to make it all better."

"Good morning, Lori, and it is good. This isn't as bad as it looks, I promise," Sarah Napier said. The sweet Southern transplant patted her arm comfortingly. "We've moved you to a new office until this can get fixed. There's a two-room unit down the hall that was available, so we're putting you in there."

Lori remembered Mac showing her that office suite. It was luxe. It was also very expensive. "I can't afford that." Just when everything had been going so well.

"We aren't charging you for it. You can use it at the same cost as this one."

"The benefits of small-town living," Mac whispered in her ear.

Lori took a deep breath and then another one. She could live with that. The new office was two doors away. "Okay. Let's finished getting everything moved. Then I'll go home, shower, and be back for the open house. Is the open house still on?" she asked. She hadn't had time to prepare much for any visitors. Gloria had helped her designed a few flyers to get her started and Emily had directed her to Butterlicious Bakery so she could order six dozen cookies to go with her table of canned drinks. She had a few diplomas and certificates to hang on the wall, but that was all. It wasn't that big of an office.

"It's still on, and you'll be good to go. I'll put a sign on the door directing people to your new location," Sarah promised.

It didn't take long to move the rest of her office. But it was a mess in the new location. She didn't have enough furniture to fill the large space, and her frames were on the floor leaning against the wall. "This looks so unprofessional. Maybe I should back out of the open house," Lori moaned. The cookies and drinks could provide her with a month's worth of lunches. Then she wouldn't have to face the public. She needed another day, or a week. A month. She could be ready in a month.

But no. She had a boyfriend with a toolkit in his truck and a nice building manager who was hustling hard to ensure she had a successful office to show off.

Mac hung her picture frames, and Sarah helped her arrange her furniture and prepared an area for the goodies Lori had for her guests. She had just enough time for Mac to drive her home so she could shower, change, and return with the food.

She ran out of cookies in the first ninety minutes, but the folks who came by later didn't seem to mind. The real estate agency next door was the one handling the sales of the new cottage development, and they sent half a dozen people her way. She didn't book any appointments, but she had a list of people who'd asked her to contact them after the Independence Day weekend.

A few familiar faces also stopped by. Gloria popped in over her lunch break and gave her a thumbs-up and a promise to get together to discuss her sudden change of career plans.

Emily was a delightful pain about it. "So much for my free bed when I'm in Minneapolis. When we talked about making it big, I thought I'd be graduating to a spare room in your penthouse," she teased. The actress was very well dressed in a gorgeous sundress and strappy sandals, looking ready for a beach photo shoot instead of a casual day off.

"I am sorry about that. Truly. But maybe you'll be

able to afford to rent your own penthouse with all the acting jobs you'll be getting. If you got the commercial," Lori hinted.

"Oh, I got it," Emily exclaimed. "I got them all. I'm going national, baby! I am the new spokesperson for Career Finder."

Lori squeezed her friend in a hug so tight Emily squeaked. They'd been right. Good things happened when a person took risks. Emily's had paid off. "Tremendous news! That deserves a proper celebration. I don't even have a cookie to offer you."

"We'll do it later. Now that you're an official, full-time citizen of Holiday Beach, we can see each other any time we want. When you aren't being all lovey-dovey with Mac," Emily said. She looked at the people milling around the building. "Speaking of the man, where is he? I thought he'd be here cheering you on."

Lori had noticed his absence, but she'd been too busy to follow up on it. She'd assumed he was on his way, but now that Emily pointed it out, it was odd. Mac wouldn't abandon her. She checked her phone, but she hadn't missed a call or a text. "I don't know. I'm sure he'll be here soon. You know that he's my biggest booster." She snickered as an image popped into her head. "He's probably out there somewhere, talking about me to some poor person who has no idea they even need an architect."

Emily hugged her goodbye. "I'm so glad you're here. Will we see you tomorrow?"

That was a question Lori had heard often in the last few days. Mac had been excited when she made her decision. He'd hit ecstatic when he realized she'd be in Holiday Beach for the biggest part of the summer. He warned her to not even think about working on the Fourth of July. They had plans. Which apparently included everything on the town's celebration schedule. He promised to welcome her back with a bang, starting at dawn.

But that was a day away. Today was only the third. Where was he?

CHAPTER 33

THERE WERE MORE people on his property. They were fully loaded with hard hats, mallets, posts, and flags. One guy even had a chainsaw. Mac dropped the bouquet on his kitchen counter and stormed through his back door.

He didn't have time for this. He was already late to pick up Lori. He'd never tell her, but he had Sarah Napier reporting regularly on how she was doing. Mac knew Lori was capable and could handle herself. He just wanted to be sure she had a good grand opening. Which was supposed to culminate with him arriving with a big celebratory bouquet for opening her office and then whisking her off to dinner. But the strangers in his backyard were in the way!

"Hello? Can I help you?" He left the "leave" unsaid.

The tanned man in the white button-down shirt stepped forward. He was Mac's age, maybe a year or two older, with blond hair and blue eyes, and grinned broadly. "Hi. I'm Ben Ackerman. I bought the house next door."

"Hi, Ben. I'm Mac Mackenzie. You're on the other

side of the prop—" He stopped dead when he recognized one of the other men with him. "Hey, Patrick."

"Hi, Mac. We're resetting the property line markers since the Parkmans pulled them all out after the last time we did it," the county assessor said.

Ben approached him cautiously. "I've done my research. The previous owners seem to have left behind a reputation. I'm hoping to start on a better foot." He extended his hand.

Mac didn't have a choice. He couldn't snub the guy just because his predecessors were jerks. "Welcome to the neighborhood," he said as they shook.

"We'll be off your property as soon as it's marked. I'll give you a heads-up when I start any major construction, but for now, I've got to undo a bunch of half-completed projects. The place has good bones, but..." Ben shook his head.

"Are you looking at adding an in-ground pool?" Mac asked, attempting to figure out how much more construction he was in for.

Ben's eyebrows hit the brim of his ball cap. "Are you kidding? With the lake right there? I've got a slip at the marina for my boat for when I need my water fix."

That was good to know. "I'll be seeing you there too, then." He grinned. This was more like it. A reasonable neighbor and a potential fishing buddy as well. "When will you be moving in?"

Ben raised his hands. "That depends on what the engineer says. I wish I could get my hands on the original plans for this place."

"I think I know someone who can help with that."

He was a full thirty minutes late by the time he arrived

at Baker Residential and Commercial Designs. Lori looked exhausted, but pleased with herself. A few strands of hair had come out of her bun, and she had a streak of pen down the side of her palm. But she was smiling when he arrived, and it only got bigger when she waved at her office.

He'd been worried she hadn't had enough time to be prepared for the open house and get all her ducks in a row. Apparently her ducks were well-trained military fowl and lined up on command.

"Look!" she ordered. The snack table was empty, she was out of flyers, and she had a row of Post-its stuck to her desktop.

"I take it the open house went well," he said.

"I talked to six people. Six!"

"Is that good?" he asked hesitantly. She'd been there for four hours.

"It's excellent. Three of them gave me their contact information so I could email them next week."

"You're going to have a busy week," he said as he pulled out a card and handed it to her.

"What's this?"

"I met my new neighbor. He said he was looking for a set of the original floor plans for the Parkman place. I told him I knew a guy." He expected a thank-you, maybe a kiss. Instead, all the color drained out of Lori's face. Mac strode forward and wrapped his arm around her waist. "What? What's wrong?"

She waved the card. "Do you know who this is?"

"Ben Ackerman. Seems like a nice guy."

"And?"

"He has a boat? We only spoke for a couple of minutes. I don't know his life story."

"That's okay. I do. Your new neighbor is Benjamin Ackerman the Fourth. Of the Chicago Ackermans."

He shrugged.

She gasped. "They own the Springfield Legion Base-ball team. And Ackerman Field," she continued. When he shook his head, Lori tried one more time. "His family also owns Ackerman Athletics. That's where you get your fishing gear in Minneapolis, according to all the packaging in your boat."

"That Ackerman?"

"Yes!"

"He wants to talk to you, so please contact him next week."

"I will."

"But until then, you're all mine. Are you ready to go?" He'd taken the entire three-day weekend off. He wasn't going to look at a paint can or even a sheet of drywall. He was on vacation, his girlfriend had just moved back to town, and he was going to make the most of every single second.

"I just have to lock the door."

"Then let's go and get started on celebrating your Independence Day!"

CHAPTER 34

Boom!

Lori jumped to her feet and darted to the window, dodging boxes and chairs. She whipped back the curtain as a few sparkles fell in the pre-dawn sky. Somebody had set off a firework before sunrise. It was a good sign of the Independence Day party spirit being alive and well in Holiday Beach. It was a little early for her, though.

Two hours later, she was digging into a stack of French toast triangles and dunking her turkey bacon into the extra syrup. "What's the plan today? Fishing?"

Mac blew her a kiss from the other side of the booth. Actually, it was a raspberry, but she'd already kissed him hello, so she let it slide.

"The entire town is one big party today, so you get to take your pick." He slipped a schedule across the table. There had been a stack at the front door, and as Lori looked around the restaurant, every table was scouring their own copy.

Both sides of the sheet were full.

The bandstand at the beach had a full lineup all day

long and into the evening when the fireworks started. That's all the schedule said—fireworks. But according to everybody in earshot, the exploding display of light and color was what every other event built toward.

The waitress warmed her coffee twice before she finished her cold breakfast since everyone she'd met in town stopped by their table to say hi.

The Phams paused on their way in. Shelly ducked behind her mother, but June was excited to talk to her. The young teenager vibrated with excitement as she told them, "Everybody at my sleepover thought my room was really cool. My friend Olivia is talking to her parents because she wants to paint her room the same way, but everybody knows I did it first. Thanks for talking my mom into it. The colors are the absolute best!"

Mac introduced her to Aaron, the sheriff, and his son Trevor. "Trevor helped me clear the lot last fall so we could get the foundation dug before the winter. He was a whiz with the chainsaw."

"He's heading to Woodlands Trades Institute in the fall to study woodworking," Aaron bragged, sounding every bit like a proud papa. But his radio squawked before he could continue, much to Trevor's obvious relief.

Tripp stopped at their table as he made the rounds of his patrons. "I've been instructed by Aiden to invite you down to the beach for the air mattress race at noon and to let you know that he isn't grounded anymore and has permission to be out on the water."

"Air mattress race?" Lori asked.

"It's one of the events today. Any kid with a life preserver and floatie can enter the race. They have to make it from the starting line to the finish line using only kicking or hand-paddling power," Tripp explained.

"Mostly, it's a way to give them something to do in the water and tire them out for the afternoon."

"We'll try to make it," Mac said, "but I'm taking Lori to the carnival first. Now that she's a permanent resident of Holiday Beach, she has to take at least one spin at Goldie's Tombola."

Tripp laughed in agreement. "It is in the town's bylaws. I'll tell Aiden you wish him well and will try to be there."

After he left, Lori stared at Mac. "Carnival? Goldie's Tombolo? What are you signing me up for, Mackenzie?" He hadn't said a word about their plans for the day. Now she wondered why.

"It's nothing insidious, I swear. The carnival is a bunch of games and activities sponsored by local businesses. It's something to do outside on Independence Day that the whole family can participate in. They run it in the parking lot behind City Hall in the morning and it's over by lunch. Then the beach activities run through the afternoon."

"What's a tombolo?"

"Tombol-a," he said. "It's like a cross between a lottery and bingo. You pay for a ticket. The seller draws one out of the drum and reads the number on it. Certain tickets, like all the ones ending in zero, win a prize."

"Where did you come up with something like that?"

"Goldie Daye, Owen's grandfather, bought it in England years ago from some retired detective inspector. It's a thing over there."

"That sounds like fun," she admitted, waiting for the catch.

"You'd think. But Goldie Daye has been running it for about twenty years. He saves the worst things he finds while he hunts for antiques for his store and donates them as prizes. They're all terrible. It's tradition."

Lori snickered. "Have you won anything?"

"You know that plaque we have in the office that says "This is bananas" and has two plastic bananas glued to it?"

She nodded. It was glaringly out of place in the spartan office. It was embarrassingly bad but still funny.

"That was the prize Doug won last year. The rule is you must display the item for at least a year before you can donate it back to Goldie."

She gasped. "I love that idea. We're definitely doing that!" It would be a great way to announce to everybody that she embraced being part of her new town.

"We should get going, then."

The parking lot was a hive of activity. Most of the stalls were crowded as kids tried to throw rings over bottles to win small plastic toys or paid a dollar for three chances to drop the volunteer into the dunk tank.

Owen Daye was manning the tombola, with a pint-size assistant on a chair beside him and an elderly gentleman sitting behind the prize table. "Step right up and try your luck. You there, lovely lady, how would you like to win any of these amazing prizes?" He gestured to the table where an assortment of astounding artifacts was on display. A wind chime made from collector's teaspoons, a ceramic drooling alien cookie jar, and an unused 2002 desk calendar were in the first row.

"Those are indeed amazing prizes," Lori agreed. They were ridiculous and she couldn't wait to display one in her new office. She handed Owen a five-dollar bill. "I'd like to take my chances, please."

Rather than spinning the barrel and pulling out five

tickets at once, Richie insisted on cranking the handle until the barrel spun by itself and slowed to a stop, and then pulling out a single ticket before doing it again. The little boy drew five non-winners in a row.

Lori handed over another five. "Let's do it again."

The odds said she should have one winner out of ten, but again, she came up empty.

Then Lucy stopped by the table. "How's she doing, Owen?"

The antique dealer shook his head. "No luck."

Lucy dropped a single dollar bill on the table, nodded at them, and walked away.

"What was that?" Lori asked.

"Lucy can't buy a lottery ticket for herself. But she has tremendous luck when it comes to other people. Do you want to go one more time, or should we save it for the next player?" Owen asked.

"I don't know. I already won a weekend vacation from her. Let's save that dollar for the next person, and I'll buy my own tickets." She was running low on funds, but she could try again.

"Thirteen's the charm," Owen shouted as Richie finally pulled a number that ended in a zero. He directed her to the prize table, where his grandfather matched the ticket to the prize. "I hope you get hours of enjoyment from this unique art piece," Goldie managed to say with a straight face.

"It's exquisite. I'm sure I will." Lori proudly accepted the taxidermied squirrel with the boxing gloves facing off against the rubber wrestler in the toy ring.

She was stopped by half the town on her way back to Mac's truck as everyone congratulated her on her win.

Some of them tried not to laugh, but most of them gasped out the words between fits of giggles.

"I guess I'm officially part of the town now," she said as she set it carefully on the back seat.

"You sure are."

Lunch was slightly less exciting but tasty as they enjoyed grilled burgers and pop in the fresh air. They spent the afternoon on Mac's deck, enjoying the beautiful weather and avoiding the crowds. Lori appreciated it. She'd had a hectic week. Even the little time she'd spent with Mac had been filled with planning and moving. They hadn't had time to just be together in over a week.

They rejoined the party in town after supper. Tripp and Habibah had staked out a slice of grass. Their little guy was already asleep in his own miniature lawn chair, wearing a set of protective earwear. Mac set up their chairs on one side, and his friend Josh settled in place on the other side. The gazebo fell silent as the last band of the day cleared out. The gathering crowd created an audible but mild buzz as folks gathered and claimed spots to watch the anticipated show.

The lights in the park went out, and soon the area was only lit by the glow of streetlights and the moon. Mac wrapped his arm around her and pulled her close. "I did a little research. Do you know that it's our anniversary? We met for the first time six months ago today."

Her heart warmed when she realized he'd remembered. She wasn't going to say anything because she hadn't made the best first impression. "When I told the delivery people to back up in your driveway, and they dumped their loads in it instead?"

"That's the day. We've come a long way. But I was right about you, even back then."

The first firework shot into the air, leaving a white streak on the dark night sky. A trio of booms followed, with blue and red streaks taking the same path, but Lori only had eyes for Mac. "Back then, you were convinced my middle name was Trouble because that's all I caused."

"And I was absolutely correct," Mac said. "I was just wrong about what kind of trouble."

Oohs and aahs surrounded them, but the crowd seemed a million miles away. "What kind of trouble am I?" Lori asked.

He pulled her close until they were nose to nose. Then he kissed her, and the world exploded around them in a million sparkles and falling stars. "The very best kind."

THE END

ALSO BY ELLE RUSH

SWEET CONTEMPORARY ROMANCE
Holiday Beach (also available in print)

Shamrocks and Surprises

Pumpkins and Promises

Tinsel and Teacups

Fireworks and Frenemies

Hopewell Millionaires

Doctor Millionaire

Fall a Million Times

A Million Love Notes

Royal Oak Ranch

The Cowboy and the Movie Star

The Cowboy and the Pastry Princess

The Cowboy and the Constable

North Pole Unlimited

Decker and Joy

Hollis and Ivy

Nick and Eve

Rudy and Kris

Ben and Jilly

Frank and Ginger

North Pole Unlimited Collection (also available in print)

Collection 1 - Decker and Joy, Hollis and Ivy

Collection 2 - Nick and Eve, Rudy and Kris

Collection 3 - Ben and Jilly, Frank and Ginger

Resort Romances

Cuban Moon

Mexican Sunsets

Dominican Stars

Mayan Midnights

Complete series 4-book box set

COOKBOOKS
Heartmade Collection

Brunch

Mains and Sides

Holiday Table

ABOUT THE AUTHOR

Elle Rush is a contemporary romance author from Winnipeg, Manitoba, Canada. When she's not travelling, she's hard at work writing books which are set all over the world. From Hollywood to the house next door, her heroes will make you swoon and her heroines will have you laughing out loud.

Elle has a degree in Spanish and French, barely passed German, and has flunked poetry in every language she ever studied, including English. She also has mild addictions to tea, yarn, bad sci-fi movies, and HGTV.

Keep up with Elle's updates and new releases by subscribing to her newsletter at www.ellerush.com/newsletter.